To Wed a Sheik

TERESA SOUTHWICK

DESERT BRIDES

S0-AEB-182

SILHOUETTE *Romance*®

Published by Silhouette Books

America's Publisher of Contemporary Romance

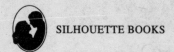 SILHOUETTE BOOKS

ISBN 0-373-19696-2

TO WED A SHEIK

Copyright © 2003 by Teresa Ann Southwick

"Kamal," Ali breathed. "I can't think when you kiss me like this."

He smiled. "I am glad." He brushed his lips to her neck and heard her gasp. "Tell me that my touch does not make you want more."

"Kamal—I don't know if this is right."

"Of course it is."

"For you, maybe. But I'm not so sure about me," said Ali.

"Then let me show you that this is right for both of us."

"Without regard for tomorrow?" she asked. "I just can't."

He let out a long breath as he released her hand, letting her go. She hurried down the hall.

Kamal closed the door, then walked into the living room. He had hoped by this time to have his feelings for the American nurse under control. But if anything, he was falling more under her spell.

Dear Reader,

Egad! This month we're up to our eyeballs in royal romances!

In *Fill-In Fiancée* (#1694) by DeAnna Talcott, a British lord pretends marriage to satisfy his parents. But will the hasty union last? Only time will tell, but matchmaker Emily Winters has her fingers crossed and so do we! This is the third title of Silhouette Romance's exclusive six-book series, MARRYING THE BOSS'S DAUGHTER.

In *The Princess & the Masked Man* (#1695), the second book of Valerie Parv's THE CARRAMER TRUST miniseries, a clever princess snares the affections of a mysterious single father. Look out for the final episode in this enchanting royal saga next month.

Be sure to make room on your reading list for at least one more royal. *To Wed a Sheik* (#1696) is the last title in Teresa Southwick's exciting DESERT BRIDES series. A jaded desert prince is no match for a beautiful American nurse in this tender and exotic romance.

But if all these royal romances have put you in the mood for a good old-fashioned American love story, look no further than *West Texas Bride* (#1697) by bestselling author Madeline Baker. It's the story of a city girl who turns a little bit country to win the heart of her brooding cowboy hero.

Enjoy!

Mavis C. Allen
Associate Senior Editor

Please address questions and book requests to:
Silhouette Reader Service
U.S.: 3010 Walden Ave., P.O. Box 1325, Buffalo, NY 14269
Canadian: P.O. Box 609, Fort Erie, Ont. L2A 5X3

Books by Teresa Southwick

Silhouette Romance

Wedding Rings and Baby Things #1209
The Bachelor's Baby #1233
*A Vow, a Ring, a Baby Swing #1349
The Way to a Cowboy's Heart #1383
*And Then He Kissed Me #1405
*With a Little T.L.C. #1421
The Acquired Bride #1474
*Secret Ingredient: Love #1495
*The Last Marchetti Bachelor #1513
**Crazy for Lovin' You #1529
**This Kiss #1541
**If You Don't Know by Now #1560
**What If We Fall in Love? #1572
Sky Full of Promise #1624
†To Catch a Sheik #1674
†To Kiss a Sheik #1686
†To Wed a Sheik #1686

*The Marchetti Family
**Destiny, Texas
†Desert Brides

Silhouette Books

The Fortunes of Texas
Shotgun Vows

Silhouette Special Edition

The Summer House #1510
   "Courting Cassandra"
*Midnight, Moonlight
   & Miracles* #1517

TERESA SOUTHWICK

lives in Southern California with her hero husband, who
is more than happy to share with her the male point of
view. An avid fan of romance novels, she is delighted to
be living out her dream of writing for Silhouette Books.

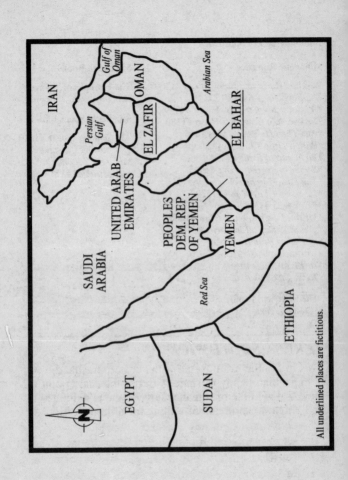

All underlined places are fictitious.

Chapter One

It was just as easy to love a rich man as a poor man. If one was looking for love.

Ali Matlock wasn't. At least not right now. She'd decided to take a break from romance and concentrate on her career. So she'd traveled halfway around the world from Texas for the job opportunity of a lifetime. She was working in a hospital built by a sheik who definitely fell into the rich-man category. She could earn triple the average stateside salary for a nurse. And the best part was the opportunity for adventure in magical, mysterious, mystical El Zafir.

As she inventoried supplies and equipment at the nurses' station in the Labor and Delivery Department, she heard the third-floor elevator doors whisper open. Kamal Hassan, the country's crown prince and the sheik who'd just crossed her mind, stepped out. He was elegantly handsome in his designer suit. Probably out of it, too.

Not that she would ever know. Although five months

ago he'd kissed her in the moonlit palace garden. But history had taught her to be wary of men—especially a sheik who kissed an engaged-to-be-engaged woman.

He stopped to speak with one of the workmen putting finishing touches on the recently completed hospital, giving her a chance to study him. With every last dark, wavy hair in place, the prince was approximately six feet two inches of tall, dark and handsome. Black eyes smoldered with intensity in an arresting face featuring a straight aristocratic nose, carved cheekbones and olive skin. He had a wonderfully shaped mouth, and boy, did he know how to use it. The memory made her heart skip at the same time she reminded herself to beware of princes wearing designer suits.

She'd met his formidable aunt, Princess Farrah Hassan, in January when the woman had visited the Texas E.R. where Ali worked. The woman had been visiting Sam Prescott, of Prescott International, a wealthy friend of the family. While there, she'd experienced chest pain that turned out to be nothing. Farrah had insisted Ali accept an all-expense-paid trip to El Zafir in March to talk about a job in the hospital her nephew was building. It had been impossible to refuse the woman even though Ali had no intention of accepting the position. She'd attended an international charity auction hosted by El Zafir.

Although enchanted by the job and the country, she'd refused the Princess's offer. Because at the time she'd been in love. Past tense. Past history. Past caring. Now she was only interested in her career. By God, if she couldn't have love, there would be adventure. Wasn't it handy that she could combine the two in El Zafir? Career and adventure, that is.

And she couldn't shake the uncomfortable feeling

that a key player in her adventure was standing a couple of feet away. Because of that kiss? Her stomach jitterbugged when she remembered what his lips had felt like against her own. But she would bet he hadn't given her a single solitary thought since that night. It was highly unlikely he even remembered her name. Why would he? She was from the wrong side of the tracks by American standards—way off the royal radar. Which begged the question—why *had* he kissed her?

He finished his conversation, then looked in her direction. "Hello."

"Your Highness," she said, clutching her pen until her knuckles turned white.

He walked toward her and stopped, his gaze never leaving hers. The scent of his aftershave drifted over the stack of boxes separating them. That and the clipboard on top of the stack was all that stood between her and the heat of his body. Her palms started to sweat.

"It's nice to see you again, Alexandrite."

She winced. "Thank you, I think. Remind me not to underestimate your powers of recalling inconsequential details, like a name no one should be burdened with."

"On the contrary. Your given name is lovely. A jewel, is it not?"

She nodded. "But Ali is so much simpler."

"On the contrary. Ali, I think, is very complicated." He held her gaze for another thundering heartbeat, then glanced around. "What do you think of it?"

"The hospital? In a word? Awesome."

On her first day of work, she'd received an in-depth tour. Now she recalled the lobby with the marble pillars and walkways, cherry-wood information and reception desks. The ground floor contained the emergency room, lab and X-ray. The second floor housed administrative offices. From there up were patient rooms and an ICU filled with the most advanced equipment money could buy. It was a seven-storied, high-tech marvel.

"A good word. Most appropriate," he answered, one black eyebrow lifting as he smiled.

Pride outlined the set of his mouth and shone in his eyes as he looked around again. Following his gaze, Ali could understand why. The brightly lit circular nurses' station was designed with technology as well as efficiency in mind. Cozily decorated labor rooms surrounded it. Serviceable low carpet covered the floor, and the hallway to her right led to comfortable patient rooms. She was impressed by the facility, but the elevators had her atwitter, agog, amazed. They were framed in gold. She couldn't decide whether or not it was the fourteen-carat variety, but that wasn't out of the question.

The royal family of El Zafir had more money than God—or so she'd heard. The expensive decorating statement might have bothered her except rumor also had it that the prince had cut no corners in his quest to build this facility. He was determined to bring his country in line with Western medical technology, knowledge and research in order to give his people the finest health care. It bordered on obsession and Ali wondered why.

On her last visit, she'd talked extensively with Princess Farrah, but his aunt had never confided the reasons, if there were any, for the crown prince's fixation. After his aunt failed, he had tried to persuade Ali to accept the job offer, but she had turned him down also. Then.

"My aunt informed me just this morning that you'd

arrived.'' The full intensity of the prince's black-eyed gaze rested on her.

''A week ago,'' she confirmed, settling her palm over her abdomen.

''You've met the director of nurses?'' he asked, frowning slightly.

Ali nodded. ''I like her very much.''

''I regret we were compelled to hire someone else in the position first offered to you. But when you refused me—''

''I'm delighted that there was still an opening on staff, Your Highness. The position as nurse-manager of Labor and Delivery is a terrific opportunity.''

''You are not disappointed you'll be unable to add something more prestigious to your résumé? As I recall, you found *that* tempting.'' A gleam stole into his eyes as one corner of his mouth curved up.

Her pulse skipped at the implication she hadn't found him intriguing. She wasn't about to share that his kiss could tempt a spinster out of her bloomers. But he probably already knew. After all, he had a reputation as an international playboy.

She stuck her hands in the pockets of the white lab coat she wore over green scrubs. ''Truthfully, I was a little nervous about that job.''

''I do not understand. Your references are most impressive. You have a master's degree in nursing, do you not?''

Again his memory for details surprised her. ''Yes. A five-year nursing program. But a degree is no substitute for experience. When I get to the top of my profession, I'll need both.''

''When?'' His eyes were keen with intelligence and amusement. ''You're certain of the future?''

She shrugged. "I've studied and worked hard. I'm good at what I do. Princess Farrah insisted I was ready now. I like to think she's right. But I believe she offered the job to me because it's difficult to get good help to come halfway around the world. I know my age could be a problem. At twenty-five, I'd have difficulty commanding respect from a staff of nurses who probably would have a great deal more practical training."

"My father ascended the throne of this country at the same age."

"That's different."

"Indeed," he said, slipping his hands into the pockets of his slacks. "The director of nurses is child's play by comparison."

"Maybe compared to running a country. But still a challenge," she said, struggling to keep the defensive edge out of her voice.

"I don't dispute it. And I do not underestimate what you do. My country does not have enough health-care professionals to adequately staff the hospital. No matter how generous the compensation, you're right that it's difficult to find skilled, qualified and highly trained personnel willing to uproot their lives and come here to work. I am in your debt."

She had no life to put on hold, and since her mother's death a year ago, no family to leave behind. Except a father who wouldn't miss her since he'd turned his back on her long ago.

"I'm looking forward to all the challenges of the job."

"My aunt has every faith in your ability to handle it in an exemplary manner."

"Princess Farrah is very kind."

"And apparently more persuasive than I. Since she convinced you to accept a job in El Zafir after all."

Ali absently twisted the cap on her pen. "Actually, I changed my mind about the job. I contacted her a few weeks ago to inquire about a position. She very kindly offered me a different one."

"Your fiancé must miss you." His voice held the barest hint of a question.

She stared up at him, noting his serious, interested air. For goodness' sake, the man was a king-in-training. Didn't he have more important things to remember than what she'd said almost half a year ago? "My fiancé?"

"Indeed. You mentioned an engagement the night I escorted you to the charity auction. If I remember correctly, your exact words were that your fiancé would not jump up and down with joy if you took a nursing position halfway around the world."

He remembered correctly and way too much, Ali thought grimly. Unfortunately, she'd discovered after returning home that she and Turner Stevens, M.D., had not been on the same matrimonial wavelength.

"As it turns out, Your Highness—"

"Call me Kamal."

She blinked. "That doesn't seem appropriate."

"In private, as we are now, it's perfectly permissible. And if I wish, it will be so."

"Kamal," she said, testing the name on her tongue. She wondered if he always got everything he wished for. If so, it must be good to be the crown prince. Because if he was trying to be a regular guy, it wasn't working. There would always be a line in the sand between him and someone like her.

And the whole behavior-with-royalty thing was foreign to her frame of reference. Did private mean just the two of them? That certainly wouldn't happen often—if at all.

"As it turns out—"

"What?" he prompted.

She sighed. "News of my engagement was greatly exaggerated."

"Oh?"

"I turned down your job offer on the assumption that the man I'd been dating for a very long time was ready to propose."

"And did he?"

Anger and pain joined with embarrassment, then formed a gigantic knot in her stomach. She briefly thought about fibbing, but decided against it. Lying to a future king could never be a good thing.

"Yes, he proposed. Just not to me."

His dark eyebrows pulled together over black eyes brimming with something that looked a lot like male satisfaction. She was about to tell him what he could do with it.

"So the jackal's idiocy is El Zafir's gain?"

Then again, he did have a way with words. "What a lovely thing to say."

"As it turns out," he said, paraphrasing her, "I do know you well after all."

She recalled him saying she wouldn't have come all the way to visit his country if the employment offer was out of the question. She'd challenged his assumption that he knew her so well. But he'd been right. Even formidable Princess Farrah couldn't have persuaded her to visit if she hadn't been interested in the opportunity. Had she subconsciously known that a marriage proposal wasn't in the cards for her? No. If she had, she wouldn't have been so completely blindsided by the betrayal. And it wouldn't have hurt so deeply.

"How nice that one night's acquaintance gives you insight into what makes me tick."

The words came out sharper than she'd intended. It wasn't fair, or especially bright, to take out her frustration on the crown prince of an oil-rich, up-and-coming nation.

"So, what brings you here today?" she asked, trying to change the subject. It wasn't quite as transparent as "nice weather we're having," but close.

His chin rose a fraction and his black eyes narrowed. "I am here *every* day."

Then why hadn't she seen him before this? Maybe because his aunt had *just* told him of her arrival? What a difference a four-letter qualifier made. A glow started inside her but she shut it down stat. Her idea of adventure was traveling to an exotic land. It did not include falling for a guy who would kiss a woman he'd thought was engaged. She was too smart for that. Once burned, twice shy.

"I see." She picked up the clipboard on the stack of boxes between them. "It was nice to see you again, Kamal. But if you'll excuse me, I've got a lot of work to do."

He nodded. "I will do my best to make your stay in El Zafir everything you hope."

"Thank you."

As she watched him walk away, she couldn't help wishing his shoulders weren't quite so broad and his stride not quite so long. Because rich man, poor man, beggar man, thief—it made no difference. Loving any man wasn't easy. Period.

Not that their paths would cross. He ran a country.

She'd been hired to run the maternity ward of his hospital. And if that wasn't enough to convince her, not a single research source she'd consulted about El Zafir had ever promised that Ali's foreign adventure would include a dalliance with a handsome prince.

Ali Matlock was a distraction.

Kamal knew because his meeting had dragged on longer than it should have. And the fault was hers. The ministers of finance and education had repeated information two and three times because thoughts of the attractive American had splintered his concentration. It was a weakness he would take pains to overcome.

He looked at his watch as he left the palace business wing and hurried to the family quarters. No doubt he'd missed Johara's prenatal checkup. His sister was eight months pregnant, an unfortunate result of her teenage rebellion. After the first angry confrontation, the king had ignored his daughter. And the baby's jackal of a father had the audacity to be killed in a motorcycle accident before Kamal could take him apart with his bare hands, then force what was left of him to marry his sister. Instead, Kamal had given her his promise that she could lean on him. Always.

Today he hadn't exactly broken his promise. But he'd certainly bent it.

He stopped before the door to his sister's suite of rooms and knocked. When his aunt bade him enter, he did so, grateful the older woman had been there for his sister.

Following the sound of female voices, he crossed the marble foyer and entered the living room. Along with his two sisters-in-law, Penny and Crystal, he found Farrah on the semicircular sofa that dominated the room.

"Has the doctor been here?" he demanded of his aunt.

Holding a delicate china cup, she looked up at him. She was an elegantly attractive woman in her fifties, although she could pass for twenty years younger. Her black eyes snapped with intelligence in her unlined face. Black hair, expertly coiffed, turned under and brushed the collar of her jewel green silk suit jacket. "Yes."

"Been and gone," Penny informed him. "He apologized for not waiting for you. But he had to get back to the hospital."

This small, delicate, blond, blue-eyed American had captured his youngest brother's heart when she'd been assigned as his assistant. The family charmer, Rafiq had been charmed by her and they quickly married. Although her slender figure didn't show it yet, they were expecting a child within the year.

"I was delayed," he explained.

"A likely story," Crystal said, her hazel eyes twinkling. "I think you would grab any excuse to avoid a chick thing."

"Chick thing?" he asked.

"You know." Crystal's grin betrayed the fact she was baiting him. "Prenatal care, babies, swollen ankles, water retention."

"Ah," he said, permitting himself a small smile.

He'd once thought Crystal's hair nondescript. But long and loose as now, it shone with red highlights. She'd been hired as the nanny to his brother Fariq's five-year-old twins and they'd fallen in love. Looking at her rounded curves, one would never guess that she, too, would give birth to his brother's third child before the end of the year.

A fleeting twist of envy gripped Kamal before he suppressed the feeling. His brothers were second and third in line to the throne. They could afford to fall in love. He could not. He had no intention of letting any weakness distract him from his responsibilities to his country and its people. For him, marriage was strictly a duty to be undertaken, but love wouldn't be involved.

"Where is Johara?" he asked, looking around.

"In the other room," Farrah answered, lifting her chin toward his sister's bedroom.

He could hear the distant, indistinct sound of a female voice. Looking at his aunt, he asked, "What did the doctor say?"

"He wishes to see her once a week until she gives birth."

"Why?"

"It is standard procedure during the last month of pregnancy." Her smooth forehead wrinkled with worry. "One thing of concern—her blood pressure is slightly elevated. As yet, he doesn't believe it's of consequence, but instructed us to call him if we have any worries or questions."

He nodded grimly. Pregnancy and birth were the cycle of life. The most natural thing in the world. Unless there was a problem. He'd watched Johara's mother lose her life while she was with child. Pushing aside his dark thoughts, he looked at the three women sitting on the sofa—two of them with an unmistakable glow.

"May I inquire about your checkups?"

"A-okay," Penny informed him. "Morning sickness has passed and we're doing fine."

"Me, too," Crystal said. "My only hitch was on the scale. I have to cut back on dessert and beef up the protein, if you'll pardon the pun."

"Of course. Anything for a beautiful woman."

She grinned. "Kamal, you're a shameless flatterer, just like your brother. Although Fariq didn't reveal that trait at first."

Penny laughed. "That was before he saw through your disguise."

An interesting time, Kamal remembered. His aunt had gone to an exclusive agency in New York to hire a new nanny for his brother's children, preferably a plain woman who would not attract undue attention and disrupt the palace. She'd come back with two new employees who had bewitched his brothers. He realized his aunt was also responsible for bringing Ali Matlock here to work in the hospital and wondered if he should be concerned. Then he decided not to be. He had yet to meet the woman who could persuasively divert him from his duty. Ali was nothing more than a distraction; he wouldn't let her be anything more.

But he *was* expected to produce an heir. Soon. The hints from his father and aunt Farrah were getting bolder and less veiled.

Crystal sighed. "Did you know the first time I met Fariq he told me beautiful women are an unwelcome distraction?"

"No," Kamal said a little too quickly and forcefully. She couldn't know he'd just had the same thought a moment ago. But Ali had splintered his concentration, producing the weakness. Fortunately, she worked in the hospital, not the palace. It was unlikely she would distract him a second time.

Just then the sound of female laughter carried to him, before Princess Johara waddled—walked—into the room. Behind her was his own personal unwelcome distraction. Ali Matlock.

"Kamal!" His sister came forward to greet him.

He leaned down and kissed her on both cheeks. "How are you, little one?"

"Not so little." She placed her hands on her bulging belly. "Did Aunt Farrah tell you what the doctor said? My blood pressure?" she asked, her lovely dark eyes brimming with worry.

"I was informed." He looked at Ali.

She was dressed as she'd been when he'd seen her at the hospital several hours before. White lab coat over green scrubs. Women in El Zafir dressed conservatively with long sleeves, high necklines and hems that covered their legs to mid-calf. She was covered appropriately for her work, but somehow what he couldn't see tantalized him more. Her auburn hair was twisted up and off her collar, but several tendrils caressed her cheeks and flirted with her long neck. Big eyes, brown with flecks of green and gold, stared back at him.

Six months ago, he'd seen her dressed for a ball. He'd thought about her often in the intervening months and couldn't comprehend why. She was a woman just like any other. So why had he been unable to forget her?

"We meet again," he finally said.

"So we do. Since I'm managing hospital L and D, Dr. McCullough thought I should be his nurse today. He returned to the hospital, but I'm off duty and Princess Johara insisted I stay on after the house call." She looked around the suite and laughed. "Some house."

"The first time I saw the palace," Penny said, "I wanted to drop a trail of crumbs so I could find my way out."

"I hear that," Crystal agreed. "But, trust me, all the walking is good for a girl's waistline."

"Unless you're big as a house," Johara said ruefully.

"As long as there are no complications, walking is good for you in your condition. Or should I say conditions." Ali grinned at each of them in turn. "A plethora of pregnant princesses."

Everyone laughed. Including Kamal.

"You should do that more often." Ali was studying him. "Your subjects will be less likely to run screaming from the room."

"No one screams or runs from me—"

"Sometimes they do have to run." Penny stood. "This pregnant princess has an appointment with the minister of education. Please say he's going to have good news for me," she added, meeting his gaze.

"Sufficient funds have been allocated for your early childhood education program," Kamal informed her.

"Excellent." She stood on tiptoe and kissed his cheek. "I'll see you all at dinner tonight."

"Wait," Crystal said, standing. "I have to go, too. The twins will be finished with their art lesson shortly. I love seeing their drawings." She kissed his other cheek. "Bye, all. Ali it was great to meet you. I'm sure we'll be seeing you again soon."

"I'll look forward to it," she answered.

"I'm afraid I must go as well." Aunt Farrah placed her empty teacup on the table and stood. "Ali, thank you for coming. If there is anything you require while you're in the hospital's employ, I insist you let me know."

"Thank you, Your Highness."

When everyone left, Kamal was alone with only two women—one very pregnant. The other disturbed him more than she had just several hours before. The laughter she'd provoked had briefly disarmed him.

"Kamal, Ali asked me to show her around my suite. I'm so glad she's here. The doctor scared me. He said high blood pressure during my pregnancy could put the baby in danger."

"And you, too," Ali warned. "But let's not borrow trouble. It's important you stay calm."

"I was very calm," the girl said, "until he told me all the horrible things that could happen to my baby. But you made me feel better."

"I'm glad."

"If you'll excuse me for a moment, I have to—" She looked at her brother. "That is, I need to—"

"Use the bedpan—so to speak?" Ali finished for her.

"Yes!" Her eyes narrowed as she looked at her brother. "Keep Ali company. Be nice."

"I am always eminently cordial," he said. That was the second time it had been implied that his formality could be intimidating. He was merely being polite.

His sister rolled her eyes without reply, then left the room. Leaving him alone with Ali.

"I wish to know the truth," he said. "Her blood pressure? Is it serious?"

"Dr. McCullough takes pregnancy very seriously. And so do I."

"As do I. But is there danger to my sister?"

"Not immediate. Everything I said to her is absolutely true. There's nothing for you to be alarmed about."

"On the contrary. When a woman is with child there is always cause for concern. Johara's mother died from pregnancy complications. A rare condition, we were told, but she was still gone. My sister was five years old.''

''I'm sorry,'' she said, obviously shocked. ''I didn't know.''

''It was many years ago. But about my sister. She's young—merely in her teens. It would seem to me youth would be in her favor.''

''On the contrary. Teens are at high risk for PIH—pregnancy-induced hypertension. High blood pressure,'' she explained. ''If left untreated, it can cause seizures.''

''What can be done?'' he asked, struggling to keep his voice neutral.

''Bed rest. Medication if necessary. Swelling is a symptom—''

''But my sister's ankles are swollen. She often says she's retaining enough water to raise the level of the Arabian Sea.''

Ali smiled at the exaggeration. ''That's normal. Swelling in the hands and face isn't. You need to watch her for—''

Johara came back in the room pressing a hand to her lower back. ''I can't believe I will be a mother in a few short weeks. Part of me is very anxious to see my baby and hold him. But another part of me is afraid of the process of bringing him into the world.''

''You'll do fine,'' Ali assured her.

''Aunt Farrah tells me it doesn't hurt. But I don't know whether or not to believe her.''

''People tolerate pain differently,'' Ali said, cautiously diplomatic.

''She's never given birth,'' Kamal said wryly.

''Oh. That would tend to cancel out her opinion.'' Ali put her arm around Johara and led her to the sofa, then gently settled her on it. She sat down beside the teenager. "I've never had a child either, but I've been present at many births. Without firsthand experience, I can only give you my impressions. There is pain. But there are medications to help manage it. Next week when you see the doctor we can talk about those things. Knowledge is power. The more you know, the more in control you'll feel."

"I think so, too," she agreed. "What do you think, Kamal?"

"What Ali says makes a lot of sense. She's studied and worked hard in her field. You should be glad she agreed to work in our country."

"Oh, I am. But I wish—" Johara lowered her gaze to the clasped hands in her lap.

"What, little one?" he asked gently.

"I wish my mother was here."

Kamal tried to understand. He'd lost his own mother when he was but ten years old and didn't remember what it was like to rely on anyone else. Because that was the first time he'd seen his father anything but strong and in control. Five years later the king had married Johara's mother then lost her as well. He'd staggered beneath the grief of losing another beloved wife and the weakness took a profound toll. It was then Kamal had vowed love would never bring him to his knees that way.

Kamal sat on her other side and touched a finger beneath her chin, lifting her gaze to his. "If I could bring her back for you, I would in a heartbeat."

Unhappiness settled over her delicate features. "I have no father—"

"Yes, you do—"

She shook her head. "No. You heard him. When he

learned of my baby he said I am no longer his daughter.
Ever since, he has only spoken to me when absolutely
necessary and always in anger. I have shamed him and
he will never forgive me. I am worse than dead to
him.''

Kamal feared she was correct. "Give him time, Johara. Until then, know this. You are not alone. I will
be with you.''

"You are so good to me. There is something I *would*
ask,'' she said, taking his hand between her two smaller
ones.

From the time she was very little, she'd followed
him around and looked up to him. He cared deeply for
his only sister, this fragile woman/child of beauty, spirit
and fierce independence. "You have only to name your
pleasure, little sister, and I will make it so. Ask of me
anything.''

"I want Ali to move into the palace and be with me
until my baby is born.''

Anything but that.

Chapter Two

Stay in the palace?

Ali hadn't seen that one coming. Stupid, but true. She sank into the cushy plushness of the semicircular white sofa and thought, there were adventures. And there were *adventures*. It's why she'd come to El Zafir in the first place.

It's also why she'd agreed to accompany the doctor on this house call—or should she say palace call. The chance to have a gander at the inside of the royal palace was irresistible. But staying there 24–7? A girl from the wrong side of the tracks in Nowhere, Texas? That could be pushing the adventure envelope too far. She'd feel like a guppy in a garden chair.

Kamal's gaze gave no hint of his reaction to the request as he studied her. Then he looked at his sister who sat beside him. He took her hand protectively into his own.

"Johara, is that really necessary? The palace physician is here and—"

"He is not an obstetrician."

"Neither is Ali," he pointed out.

"But she works with my doctor. She understands these things and I feel comfortable with her."

"You wound me, little one. I am your brother. I wish to be here for you and I thought you were untroubled in my presence. Am I—what is that American saying?"

"Chopped liver," Ali supplied.

"Exactly. Am I chopped liver?"

"You are a man, Kamal."

Same thing, Ali thought. When he frowned, she was afraid she'd either voiced her opinion or he'd read her mind. Either way she would be toast. But he didn't say anything.

The princess rested her head on his shoulder in a conciliatory gesture. "I do not wish to offend you. But at a time like this, a woman wants another woman with her."

"You have Penny and Crystal," he said. "I'm certain it would make them happy to be available to you."

She shook her head. "They are newly married and they do not have medical training. Besides, I do not wish to intrude on their happiness."

"They are married to your brothers who are as concerned for your welfare as I."

"I do not wish to take my brothers' wives from them at a time when their focus should be on starting their new lives. And families."

Ali watched the exchange between brother and sister. The crown prince's reaction was very interesting. Until this moment, she hadn't thought royalty could sweat or squirm. Unless she missed her guess, he was darn close to doing both. But what was the problem?

Maybe it had something to do with that invisible line between royalty and commoners. He was cordial and polite, but he wanted her at a distance.

Ali held up her hand. "Excuse me, but—"

"Might I suggest Aunt Farrah?" He dropped a quick kiss on the top of Johara's dark head. "She is a single woman and has been like a mother to you since you lost your own."

"Our aunt has indeed been very good to me. But she has no personal or practical knowledge to offer on the subject of childbearing," Johara protested. "As you said, she's never had a baby."

"Nor has Ali," he said, his gaze sliding to hers.

Now *she* was starting to squirm. It might be a stretch for royalty, but peasants like herself had a great deal of experience in the art of sweating and squirming. How could she diplomatically excuse herself so brother and sister could discuss this privately? She didn't relish being on the spot and talked about as if she wasn't there.

Johara turned her big, black eyes on her brother. "As we also said, Ali is a nurse trained in labor and delivery. She's been present in that capacity at many births. She has experience. Her presence in the palace at night will calm my nerves. And the doctor said I should remain calm. Why are you hesitating, Kamal?"

A good question. Ali was wondering the same thing. He met her gaze but his own was unreadable.

"Ali has come halfway around the world and is settled in the American compound," he said. "It would be presumptuous to ask her to disrupt her life once again. Besides, the palace is farther from the hospital."

"Five minutes away," Johara protested. "Ten at the most."

Just what Ali was going to say.

"This could be an unpardonable imposition, little sister. It is not as if you have no one else to turn to."

"It can't hurt to ask her."

He leaned down and kissed his sister's cheek. "I think you should get some rest. You look fatigued."

"I am a little tired," she agreed.

"I will handle this," he said. "Go and lie down. Never fear. You will come to no harm. I will see to it."

She nodded. "Ali, thank you for staying with me. I appreciate it very much."

"You're welcome."

When his sister was gone, Kamal stood and walked to the other side of the glass-topped coffee table. "I apologize if my sister's request has made you uncomfortable."

It wasn't the request, but his attitude that made her ill at ease. But probably it wasn't appropriate to say that to a prince. Especially the prince whose pet project was the hospital where she worked. If he wanted to throw his royal weight around and fire her, who would tell him he couldn't do it?

Her world wouldn't come to an end if she lost her job, but it would put a serious speed bump in the path of solidifying her future. And what other position would afford her the adventure opportunity of a lifetime? She should let His Royal Snootiness off the hook and say thanks, but no thanks. Except she had a perverse impulse to not make it easy on him.

"Your *sister* has nothing to apologize for."

One dark eyebrow rose. "Meaning I have done something which requires an apology?"

She decided not to answer that directly. "Princess

Johara is young, pregnant and scared. She merely said she wanted me to stay with her. That in no way made me uncomfortable. It was your reaction that puzzles me. Why don't you want me here?''

"I have no feelings one way or the other. I was merely attempting to let my sister know that it is thoughtless to turn other people's lives upside down at her whim. Some are intimidated and do not realize it is permissible to refuse a request from a member of the royal family.''

"Don't worry about me. I'm not intimidated,'' she lied. "I can stand up for myself and say no.''

"Then I will tell her that you are unable to accept her invitation to live here in the palace until her baby is born.'' His tone was rife with male satisfaction and it bugged her.

"That's not what I meant. I *am* able to accept. I'm just not certain I want to.'' She had the satisfaction of surprising him. It was written all over his handsome face.

"Is that so?''

"You've presumed to know what I would do.'' What happened to her polite thanks, but no thanks? Where was this spine of steel coming from? From his mightier-than-thou attitude, that's where, she thought. "If you want to know my answer, try asking me.''

By gum, if she wanted to stay in the royal palace with his sister, she would do it.

His dark eyebrows rose and he straightened to his full height, planting his feet just a little wider apart. He reminded her of the conquering hero surveying his victory. It was a good look and he wore it well. But she couldn't help feeling it was also body language to let her know he was the boss and she hadn't backed him into a corner.

"As you wish," he said in his velvet-smooth voice. "Would you agree to my sister's request to live in the palace for several weeks until her baby arrives? Before you answer, be advised that my sister will be well taken care of if you wish to say no."

That did it. He wanted her to refuse. That pushed some major buttons. She was mistress of her fate and no one was going to make her decisions for her. "I would be happy to accept Princess Johara's invitation."

Before he could mask it, his dark eyes narrowed and his mouth compressed into a straight line. She knew as surely as if he'd said it out loud—he'd thought she would turn him down. He didn't want her to stay in the royal palace. And why should he? She wasn't royal palace material. She wasn't even the right kind of daughter material. Her own father had walked out on her and her mother to marry someone with higher social standing.

But come on. Even if Kamal knew all that ancient history about her, it had no bearing on this situation. What was his problem? This place was so big it wasn't as if they would be tripping over each other. He never had to see her. Suddenly she realized how much she wanted to stay. As adventures went, this assignment was a plum among plums. It was the crunchy chocolate coating on the vanilla ice-cream bar.

"Is my sister in imminent danger?" he asked.

"If you're asking whether or not it's really necessary for me to be in residence, the answer is no. All my presence will do is give the princess some peace of mind."

"I do not wish to interfere with the duties at the hospital for which you were hired."

"That shouldn't be a problem. As long as Johara knows I have a job to do. If she's okay with my being here after work, then I would like to accept the invitation."

"Very well, then."

"Okay." Ali nodded. Although she had no frame of reference for living in a palace. But this would undoubtedly be her only chance to experience it. And isn't that what coming here was all about? A fabulous job in an exciting country? Her situation just got more fabulous and definitely more exciting. Adventure, here I come, she thought.

And if she ran into Kamal in the hallway, he could feel free to ignore her. She would simply smile and say hello because a person could never go wrong being polite.

And if her heart beat a little faster and her palms grew damp, he would never know. And what he didn't know wouldn't hurt her. Right?

"I will inform my aunt that you will be moving into the palace."

Right.

"Something is wrong, Kamal?" Aunt Farrah sat on her pristine sofa drinking a before-dinner sherry.

"Of course not. Why do you ask?"

Behind her on the light tan-colored wall hung a tapestry depicting a scene from El Zafirian history reflecting the courageous exploits of one of his ancestors. He'd always especially liked this particular wall hanging among the many expensive paintings his father's sister collected. History was his passion. Someday he hoped to take his place with favorable marks from the historians.

"This is me," she said. "I've known you since you were born. From the time you were a small boy when there was something troubling you, the vein in your forehead began to throb. It is throbbing now."

"You're joking," he said, even as he touched that particular spot.

She merely smiled. "What is it you wish to discuss with me that couldn't wait until the family gathers for dinner in a little while?"

"Ali Matlock."

"It's about time," she murmured.

"Excuse me?"

"I said it's fine."

"What?" he asked.

"I spoke with Johara. She told me about asking Ali to stay with us in the palace until the baby is born. I think it's a splendid idea."

"Do you?" Kamal had the unsettling thought that men ruled at the pleasure of women. Power was meted out by the females around him. But surely he was mistaken.

"After what the doctor said today, it would ease my mind knowing there was a health-care professional here in the palace."

"There's a highly gifted physician in the palace at all times," he reminded her.

"True. But having a nurse whose specialty is childbirth would be a comfort to Johara. And I must admit, although the doctor's intention wasn't to alarm us, I was fairly concerned following his examination of your sister."

"As was I."

He was also intrigued by the American nurse. From the first, he'd noticed her fairness of face. Today he'd found her feisty as well. If she hadn't challenged him regarding his less-than-gracious behavior, he wouldn't find her so, but she had. Had he been testing her? Not consciously, but now he knew if she had failed, he would have cheerfully forgotten her. But she'd made that impossible. *And,* for the foreseeable future, she would be living under his roof. He had yet to decide how he felt about it.

"Kamal, did you hear me?"

"I'm sorry, Aunt. I have a matter of some importance on my mind."

"As do I. Has Ali agreed to stay?"

"Yes. She will come after work in the hospital and spend the evenings here until my sister has her baby."

There was a gleam in his aunt's eyes as she nodded. "I will have the room next to Johara's prepared."

"Very well. If there is nothing further, I will leave the details in your capable hands and see you at dinner." He started to turn away.

"Wait, Kamal. Since you're here, there is another matter I wish to take up with you."

"Yes?"

"Your father consulted with me on the matter of your wife."

"I have no wife."

She sighed. "Yes. That is the heart of what he consulted me about."

"I do not understand why it was necessary for him to discuss my marital status with you."

"Because you refuse to and he is concerned." She set her delicate crystal sherry glass on the gold-inlaid coffee table. "It is time, Kamal."

"I disagree."

"You are not getting any younger. It is your duty as crown prince to marry and produce an heir to the throne."

"I know what my duty is. But I see no reason to hurry the process."

"Your behavior is proof of that."

"To what are you referring?" he asked.

She sighed. "You are seen with many women, yet you do not seem interested in a single one of them."

Until now, he thought, remembering the way Ali's eyes sparkled with mischief during their exchange. He wished she was like all the other women he'd known.

"I do not wish to rush into anything. It is my intention that the union be enduring."

"Again I must remind you I've known you since you were a baby. There are other reasons for your hesitation. I am aware of your sensitive nature."

"Such emotion implies a weakness not permitted the man who will assume responsibility for his country's people."

"The line of succession will go to your brother's son if necessary. But that is only as a last resort. You are the crown prince. It is your obligation to try."

"And I have been, Aunt Farrah. But the woman I choose must possess certain qualities."

Shaking her head in defeat, she said, "As I said, you must do your best to produce an heir. What steps will you take toward acquiring a bride to accomplish this?"

"Do not worry, Aunt. I will do what is expected of me."

"You haven't so far. Why should I believe you will now?"

"Because my father wishes it now."

"That's true. He has charged me to see that your duty is done soon. I must inquire how you will go about finding a suitable woman to marry. If you require assistance finding someone, I could—"

"I don't." He let out a long breath as he struggled to keep a tight rein on his temper in the presence of a female who was also a revered family member.

"I wish only to help. Would you like me to compile a report of suitable candidates?" She folded her hands in her lap and stared at him.

"Choosing a wife is not unlike hiring an assistant. She must have certain qualifications and I'm perfectly capable of procuring a suitable candidate for my bride."

"As you wish," she said, her gaze never wavering from his. "But it is imperative that you understand the depth of your father's displeasure."

"I think I understand."

She shook her head. "No. But hear this. If you do not select a bride in a time frame acceptable to the king, the choice will no longer be yours."

Irritation scratched at his nerves and he fought to keep his voice neutral. "It was my understanding that arranged marriages were a thing of the past in El Zafir."

She sniffed. "Only because they have become unnecessary. But if you continue to procrastinate, the practice can easily be reinstated."

"Very well. Your message is duly noted." He swallowed his anger and the taste was bitter on his tongue.

He left his aunt and walked back to his suite of rooms to change for dinner. As a small boy his father had continuously reminded him that with great power comes great responsibility. Kamal had learned from

watching his father that weakness of emotion was an
undesirable flaw. No one understood duty better than
Kamal Hassan. He would do what was expected of
him. But before he did, he would have a final fling.
Suddenly a vision of Ali Matlock came to mind.

Chapter Three

Dinner in the royal palace, Ali decided, was like being thrown into the deep end of the pool with no working knowledge of water safety and no arm floaties to keep her from sinking. One on one with Kamal was one thing. But the whole family together in a dining room that felt as big as her entire apartment at home was intimidating.

This environment of wealth and formal beauty was so far beyond her frame of reference, she could as easily be on another planet. The soft *ting* of goldware against china was an elegant, sophisticated sound she'd seldom heard and always in a restaurant. Nothing in her nurse's training had prepared her for this. If someone choked on a crab-stuffed mushroom and became a candidate for the Heimlich Maneuver or clogged their arteries from froufrou food and needed CPR, then she was your gal.

A symptom of her intimidation was being tongue-tied. The silver lining to that was being able to observe her surroundings without interruption. If she'd been a brave little soldier who muddled forward, she wouldn't have had as much opportunity to admire the crystal chandelier overhead and the graceful wall sconces that lighted the room with just the right amount of soft glow. Nor would she have been able to appreciate the arrangements of fresh flowers on the table and every other flat surface in the room.

She admired the intricate pattern on the crocheted lace tablecloth and suspected it cost a small fortune. Only the imminent threat of dehydration could compel her to move a hand anywhere near liquid and chance a spill on the costly material. The upside: her full glasses of water and champagne would save the hovering servers the necessity of refilling them.

Ali looked at Princess Farrah who was sitting diagonally across from her at the end of a table long enough to line dance on. The woman was engaged in a spirited conversation with her nephew Rafiq and his wife, Penny, regarding El Zafir's greatest natural resource—children. King Gamil sat at the head of the table talking with Fariq and Crystal about the country's opportunities for foreign investors. Kamal was between Ali and Johara. She felt like a bump on a pickle and just about as exciting. Taking call for a teenage mother-to-be was one thing. Having dinner with a multitude of royals at the invitation of the little mother's aunt was something else altogether. What did one converse about with them?

Ali was in over her head. No question about that. Kamal was intimidating enough all by himself, although she'd managed to stand up to him. But now she was afraid to open her mouth—even with Penny and Crystal there.

In college speech class, she'd learned one of the techniques to get over stage fright was to picture the audience in their underwear. Her gaze slid sideways to Kamal. In his dark suit, tone-on-tone deep gray shirt and tie, he looked every inch the designer-dressed, powerful crown prince—a sight that made her pulse pound and her hands tremble. One thing became crystal clear to her in that moment. Picturing Kamal in his underwear wouldn't cure what ailed her. If anything, it could double-knot her tongue.

"Ali?"

"Hmm?" She glanced past Kamal's chest to his aunt's amused gaze. "I'm sorry. You were saying, Your Highness?"

"I said I'm delighted that you could accept my invitation for dinner this evening. We wanted to welcome you and make your first night in the palace memorable."

"I—I—" She cleared her throat when the word came out a croak. "I assure you, this is an experience I'll never forget," she replied sincerely.

"Is your room comfortable?" the princess asked.

"Is there anything you need?" The king looked like a gracefully aging movie star with his dark eyes and silver hair. Very Cesar Romero.

Leaving her dessert untouched, Ali settled her gold fork on the side of her delicate china plate. It seemed the prudent thing to do since she couldn't eat anything anyway.

"My rooms are wonderful," she said, picturing in her mind the large suite.

The living room had French doors leading to a balcony that overlooked the Arabian Sea. The large bedroom was littered with numerous pieces of matching cherry-wood furniture. Gold bathroom fixtures. Marble floor. What was not to like? Her rooms were definitely satisfactory—the most satisfactory rooms she'd ever had.

Johara leaned forward, looking past her brother. "I am happy you could stay. It relieves my mind to have you close. I will—"

"Farrah." King Gamil interrupted his daughter and pointedly met his sister's gaze. "Is there any progress on that matter we were discussing the other day?"

Ali glanced at the teenage princess and saw the flush that crept into her cheeks at being talked over as if she wasn't there. Her mouth compressed to a straight line as her large dark eyes snapped with what looked like resentment. Ali couldn't help feeling sorry for the young girl. But before she could dwell further on what had happened, Princess Farrah was speaking. She noticed the questioning look the woman slid in Kamal's direction.

"Kamal and I have talked. I have high hopes that things will proceed well from now on."

"Do we want to know what things?" Penny glanced at each of them, then her husband.

In response, Rafiq smiled lovingly at her. "Probably not, my dear. So I will change the subject." He looked at his sister. "Johara, how are you feeling?"

Good for him, Ali thought. Just because her father seemed bent on pretending Johara wasn't there didn't mean the rest of the males had to as well. She saw the dark look the girl tossed her father before her chin lifted.

"Big," the teen answered, staring ruefully at her belly. "I am very ready for this baby to arrive."

"I can imagine," Crystal said. "I'm barely showing, but I can hardly wait to hold this child in my arms."

Fariq looked at her. "My wife is a wonderful mother. She's proven that with Hana and Nuri."

"Your twins adore her," Penny said. "But seeing how uncomfortable Johara is, I vote we shorten the gestation period significantly."

"I'll draft a resolution," Kamal said wryly. "And submit it to the El Zafirian ruling cabinet. We'll see what we can do to accommodate your request."

"Yes," Johara agreed, shifting uncomfortably. "I second that."

The king cleared his throat. "Are you well, Crystal? Penny? I understand the doctor was here yesterday."

"Everything's fine with Penny and me," Crystal said.

Ali tried to think of something to add to this conversation. This was a subject she knew about. The king of the country had made an effort to be polite to her even if he was being an old poop to his daughter. Ali should be able to come up with a bonding sort of thing to say.

"Your Highness, you must be very excited at the prospect of having three new grandchildren here in the palace," she finally managed to say.

King Gamil turned his dark-eyed gaze on her. "I have only *two* grandchildren on the way."

Ali's heart was pounding as she saw the tears in the young girl's eyes and waited for someone to come to her defense. Crystal and Penny looked as shocked as she felt. The men stared daggers at their father, but said nothing. Ali felt the pressure build inside her. It was probably too forward, but she couldn't keep silent. Outrage melted her intimidation.

"Johara is your daughter. When she gives birth in a couple weeks, that child will be your grandchild also."

"Miss Matlock—Ali," the king said. "I do not expect you to understand this. But I no longer have a daughter."

"You can't mean that," she said. "I know her situation isn't ideal, but—"

He held up a hand. "She sits here at the insistence of her brothers and aunt. But she chose to turn her back on me when she ignored all the teachings of her revered ancestors. I cannot forgive that."

"It wasn't like that, Father." Johara slapped her napkin on the table. "I fell in love."

As if she hadn't spoken, the king took a sip of coffee from his cup, then set it back on the saucer with an almost musical clink. "Kamal, how is the hospital progressing?"

Studying the crown prince, Ali held her breath. Anger and disapproval swirled in his eyes as he met his father's gaze.

"Father," he said, "are you also aware that the doctor said Johara's pregnancy is at a very delicate stage? Her condition can be adversely affected by stress. She needs your support—"

"Her condition is that she is with child and without a husband. She has shamed me."

"But, Your Highness," Ali blurted out. Funny how adrenaline loosened the tongue. She leaned toward the man on her left. "She's young. Didn't you ever make a mistake when you were her age?"

"You are a visitor to this country and therefore cannot comprehend this situation. There are consequences for dishonorable actions."

Abruptly, Johara stood. "The king is rigid in his

beliefs. He refuses to admit that times are changing even here in El Zafir. Since I cannot convince him of this, I must concentrate all my energy on my baby.''

With all the dignity a very pregnant, very emotionally upset young woman could manage, she left the room. In her wake, a churchlike silence descended.

''Times *are* changing,'' Kamal said, the muscle in his lean cheek contracting.

You go, Kamal, she rooted silently. Sure, the girl had made a mistake, Ali thought. But she was paying for it. She was going through the most momentous experience a woman could have. Under the right circumstances—a committed couple waiting for a baby that represented the tangible result of their love—it would be joyous. Johara was facing the prospect of raising her baby alone and she was doing that under the cloud of her father's disapproval. Ali crossed her fingers in her lap, hoping the crown prince would tell him off for his lack of compassion and understanding.

''Some things are not meant to change,'' the king said.

''Father, my sister is in a most delicate condition. It is likely that your attitude is contributing to her stress and could result in harm to her and her child.''

''Do not interfere, Kamal,'' the king ordered. ''You have always been weak where she is concerned. This behavior is unacceptable for the man who would follow me on the throne of El Zafir.''

Ali noticed he wouldn't use Johara's name or call her Kamal's sister. It was as if she'd been surgically cut out of the family for him. The idea outraged her. She looked at Kamal, waiting for his comeback to his father. His eyes snapped with anger and the muscle worked in his cheek as he clenched his jaw. But he said nothing more.

Where was the conquering hero she'd seen yesterday? The one who refused to be boxed into a corner?

Kamal found Ali in the palace garden. Back and forth she marched, muttering to herself as the scent of jasmine and magnolias drifted in the air. Stars winked in the black velvet sky above but the night was moonless. The only illumination came from strategically placed spotlights and the small white lights strung in the palms and date trees clustered in the center of the lush area and around the perimeter. Flowered vines climbed the pink-tinged stucco walls surrounding the courtyard. This was one of his favorite places in the palace and he came here often for the serenity it offered.

Although not tonight, he thought, watching Ali prowl like a cat. She hadn't noticed him yet and her fevered pace made him think of an enraged kitten. But when she stopped at the end of the stone pathway and turned toward him, the furious look on her face convinced him to keep that opinion to himself.

"I have been looking for you," he said.

She hurried forward and stopped in front of him. "Is it Johara? Is she—"

He held up his hand. "I left my sister a short time ago and she was in good health."

Her chin tilted up with a somewhat defiant air. "Then you were looking for me because of what happened at dinner."

"I was," he confirmed.

She straightened to her full height and met his gaze

as a glint of steel glowed in her own. "I need to explain something to you."

"Yes?"

"I have a hard time when someone is throwing their weight around. When a person is being bullied, I will defend the underdog."

"I noticed," he said wryly.

She folded her arms beneath her breasts. In her white, long-sleeved silk dress with the midcalf hem and deep V neck, the movement gave him a most enticing view of her bosom. Normally, he took his height for granted, but at times like this, he was most grateful for it. And the fact that even in high-heeled pumps, her lack of stature gave him quite a delightful vantage point.

Color stained her lovely, high cheekbones. "I've been known to act impulsively, but, I believe, with right on my side. Like tonight, for instance."

"What about it?"

"It's wrong of your father to cut off his daughter. She mentioned the emotional exile, but until I saw it with my own eyes, I didn't quite believe her." She stared at him for a moment and the shadows in her eyes made him wonder. "Johara made a mistake," she continued. "No one, especially her, denies it. But who died and made him king?" she huffed.

"I believe that would be my grandfather."

She blinked and one corner of her lush mouth lifted. "That's not exactly what I meant."

"I know."

"If he can't be supportive, she needs him not to add stress. In fact, if he's truly disowned her, why was she at a family dinner? Why hasn't he sent her away somewhere?"

"You'd have to ask my father."

"Probably he thinks that would be too easy. If he keeps her around to ignore, every day she's an outcast reminds her of her error."

"You think he's a cruel man?"

"I think the way he's treating his only daughter is cruel."

"It's complicated." Kamal sighed. "But he loves her very much. In fact, she is his favorite."

"He's got a funny way of showing it. It's hard for me to believe he favors her."

"I didn't think you would understand. But remember, a change in attitude takes time and my father is of a different generation. He is conservative and puts a high price on family honor."

"It doesn't seem especially honorable to turn your back on family, someone you're supposed to love." There was an edge to her voice that made him wonder if she had personal reasons for her impulsive defense of his sister.

But then, she was talking about love. A complex concept and one he had been successful in avoiding. Family affection was simple and straightforward. The web of emotion between a man and woman was not. It was a maze he wished never to enter or experience.

"Love equals weakness," he said. "Look what happened to my sister in the name of love."

"And you think she's weak because she gave in to her feelings for a man?"

"I will only say that a king is not permitted to be weak."

She rested her hands on her hips, drawing his attention to the luscious curves beneath the soft material of her dress.

"What you mean is that a king can't fall in love?"

He shrugged. "It happens, but I wouldn't recommend it."

She blinked at him. "How do you stop it?"

"Strength of will." He watched her assimilate his words and expected a comment. But she merely gave a small shake of her head. "Now, about your impulsive behavior at dinner," he said.

"I won't apologize for it."

"I would not ask you to."

"If you want me to leave the palace quietly, I will. But I won't say I'm sorry for expressing my opinion—" Her eyes widened. "What did you say?"

"It's not necessary for you to apologize."

"Then why were you looking for me?"

"You defended my sister."

"And it's only fair to warn you I would do it again under the same circumstances."

"I wished to offer my thanks."

"That's not your job." Her confusion gave way to irritation. "The real question is why you didn't defend her." She held up her hand. "I know you made a token attempt, but your father ordered you to stay out of it and you did. Why?"

"You would not understand."

"Try me. I heard you tell her you would be there for her always. But when her father was dumping on her, you hung her out to dry."

Kamal studied the earnest expression on her face. She was a woman of action and would not understand the necessity of biding one's time. She would chafe at waiting for the right opportunity to step in where it was possible to do the most good. He knew winning every battle wasn't necessary as long as one was victorious in the end.

"Out of respect for my father, it was necessary to keep silent."

"And you don't see that as a weakness?"

"Unpleasant, but not weak."

"You say tomato, I say to-mah-to."

He frowned. "I don't understand."

"What we have here is semantics. I suppose we need to agree to disagree. And I promise I'll attempt to control my impulsive instincts in the future."

"Not on my account," he said.

Maybe it was her recent show of temper, but she looked quite beautiful. If impulsive behavior was responsible, he wouldn't mind seeing more.

He motioned to the bench beside them. "Would you care to sit with me?"

"I should go inside. I have to work tomorrow and I need to check on Johara."

"Just for a little while. If my sister needs anything, you will be summoned."

She nodded. "All right. It is so lovely here."

Deep pink bougainvillea along with jasmine vined up the wall behind her and formed a backdrop. *She* was lovely with her dark hair and eyes that changed from brown to almost green depending on a mood that could bring out flecks of gold. Her nose was straight and well formed. But her lips were beyond fascinating. Wide but not too wide. Full but not too full. He'd kissed her once upon a time because he hadn't been able to resist the temptation of her mouth. And he hadn't been able to forget. But not until she'd arrived in his country to work had she become an immediate distraction.

He took her elbow and guided her to the bench. Through the nearly transparent material of her sleeve, he felt the heat of her skin. His belly knotted with the need to see her and touch her without the barrier of clothing between them.

They sat side by side on the bench, close enough to feel the heat of her body without touching. The sweet fragrance of the blossoms drifted around him and he would have thought it impossible to distinguish the scent of Ali's skin. He would be wrong. Blindfolded he could find her in this perfumed garden.

"So tell me about being trained to be king," she said. "What is it like? Besides the fact that you're not allowed to fall in love."

"Like any other profession, being a monarch has its ups and downs."

"Such as?"

"Marriage."

"If you're not allowed to fall in love, how can you get married?"

He thought about the interview with his aunt earlier that evening. "An order from the king would leave me no choice. It is necessary for me to produce an heir," he explained.

"But if you can't fall in love, how can you have children?"

"Ali, I'm surprised at you. I assumed all nurses were required to take anatomy and biology."

A sheepish expression crossed her face as her cheeks charmingly pinkened. "I know about the birds and bees. It's just—"

"What?"

"I've seen a lot of babies born into all kinds of situations. Single mothers, like Johara. Couples who are thrilled to bring a new life into the world. Even couples who aren't married. But they all seemed to genuinely care about one another. It just seems wrong, somehow that procreation is condensed to biology and succession.''

''Nevertheless, that is the way of things for me.''

''Since you're not waiting for a soul mate, is there a certain time frame for this union?''

''I have been ordered to choose a bride soon, or one will be chosen for me.''

''I thought arranged marriages went out with chain mail and chastity belts.''

''As did I,'' he admitted. ''But my aunt informed me that my father grows impatient for me to select the woman who would be queen.''

''So how does one select this lucky woman? Do you walk up to someone on the street and say, ''Let me make you my queen?''

He laughed. ''No.''

''Does a royal edict go out that the crown prince is seeking a bride? Then there's the ball and at the stroke of midnight the only one to catch your eye runs out and leaves behind a glass slipper. Then all the eligible women in El Zafir should report to the palace with or without said matching glass slipper?''

''It's hardly a fairy tale,'' he said, recognizing *Cinderella* in Ali's fractured account of the story.

''How about asking all willing candidates to submit a résumé?''

Again he recalled the conversation with his aunt when he'd said that choosing a wife wasn't unlike hiring an assistant. So far he'd never employed anyone he would consider marrying. He looked into Ali's wide, beautiful, mysterious eyes and realized he had considered her for many months, but a good many of those considerations had included a soft bed and twisted sheets.

"No résumé."

"Then how do you pick? Are there qualifications?"

"Yes. It is more than a title. I have given the matter a great deal of thought, as the woman who stands by my side will help shape the destiny of El Zafir. She will be important to my country's legacy. And that is important to me."

"So it's more than tiaras and table manners."

"Indeed."

"So give. What are you looking for? I'm curious," she explained.

"The woman who will be queen must care about the people of this country. Their welfare must come first. That is at the core of everything. Someone not unattractive would be nice as she will be a public figure and much photographed. Intelligence, understanding and humor would be useful qualities. An obedient, practical female who is impervious to fairy tales would be most desirable."

A frown crossed her features, then quickly disappeared. "So this icon of femininity who's going to put an end to your days as a bachelor needs to be a cross between Mother Teresa and Princess Grace."

"You are mocking me."

"Heaven forbid," she said, pressing a hand to her chest. "But I am saying it appears your days are numbered."

"You make me sound like a condemned man."

"If the crown fits—" She shrugged. "In my country, a condemned man is permitted to pick whatever he wants for his last meal."

"I have heard that."

"In your case, I guess you'd call it a last fling."

"That is a good description." He'd had the same thought himself after speaking with his aunt.

She must have seen something in his face because she asked, "Are you planning on having a fling?"

"It crossed my mind," he admitted.

"Do women need to submit a résumé for that, too? Or do you have someone in mind?"

"As a matter of fact I do."

"Who's the lucky lady?"

"You."

Chapter Four

Ali shot to her feet and instantly regretted it as her shaking legs threatened to buckle. Had she heard him right? Or was this a difference in communication styles?

"Wh—what are you saying?"

"I wish to have an affair with you."

How did one respond to such a matter-of-fact statement? If she was interested in marriage, which she wasn't, she might be affronted that he considered her only suitable enough for a fling. So was she supposed to be flattered that the crown prince wanted to make her his mistress and say thank-you? Or tell him she wasn't that kind of girl and slap his face? No, probably not. She knew how to say international incident. But wow. For the second time that night she was speechless.

"I—I don't know how to respond to that," she finally answered.

"Just say yes." He grinned.

Her knees felt like caramel left in a double boiler too long. She realized part of her wanted to throw caution to the wind and do as he asked. How stupid was that? If she wasn't smart enough to keep her emotions in check, there was unlimited potential for a broken heart. Been there. Done that. Wasn't interested in another go-round.

On the other hand, how often did a girl like her get an offer like this? And it wasn't as if he was a troll or anything. If there hadn't been the accident of birth that had made him heir to his country's throne, he could have made a fortune in Hollywood. His dark eyes smoldered with the promise of sensual pleasure. His lean face with its high cheekbones was movie-star handsome and would pull hordes of women into theaters for a fantasy fix about what his well-shaped lips could do to them. But she already knew.

"When I was here before—" She hesitated to ask what she'd been wondering about for a long time.

"Yes?" He rose from the bench and moved in front of her, just a whisper away.

She swallowed hard, but wouldn't look past the expensive collar of his designer shirt. "Why did you kiss me?"

It was always good to be straightforward when you were stalling, she decided.

"Ali." His voice was smooth as butterscotch and twice as tempting. With his knuckle beneath her chin, he gently nudged upward, forcing her to meet his gaze. Then with one finger he traced her cheekbone and tucked an errant strand of hair behind her ear. She shivered and the corners of his mouth turned up.

"Are you truly so innocent? Do you really not know how lovely and desirable you are?"

Not desirable enough or she'd be married by now. But she had sufficient desirability for Turner Stevens, M.D., to toy with her until someone better came along. Somehow, she couldn't find the will to resent the rejection that had landed her right here, right now. Still, being used was never pleasant.

She blinked up at him. "That's a 'have you stopped beating your wife' question."

"Excuse me?"

"There's no good answer. If I say yes, I'm self-centered and egotistical. If I say no, I could be accused of fishing for compliments."

"I would be happy to compliment you," he said.

She shook her head. "You don't get it. I—"

"It is you who does not get it. I am a man who never takes no for an answer."

"A good quality in a king-to-be," she said, her eyes growing wide.

"Just so. And I feel it is only fair to warn you."

"About what?"

If possible, his eyes grew darker. "In certain things, I am not a patient man. Now is one of those times. I believe in this situation negotiation has run its course and aggressive action is required."

"What kind of action?"

"I am going to kiss you, to persuade you to my way of thinking. Afterward, I wish to hear you say yes to my proposition."

Under normal circumstances, she would have been affronted. But it was difficult to be sincerely scandalized when perfume permeated the air and the trees and shrubs sparkled with magical light. And he was looking at her as if she were the most desirable woman on the planet. His confident sexuality radiated outward, battering her in relentless waves. Later she would be outraged. Right now she was bracing for impact as his mouth lowered toward her.

When he was a whisper away, he said, "Put your arms around my neck."

She stood on tiptoe and did as he asked. Not because he'd told her to, she reasoned. Or because she was hypnotized by the dark intensity in his gaze. She simply, desperately wanted to.

She felt his hands at her waist as he settled her against him and brushed his chin along her temple. "You feel like heaven in my arms," he murmured into her hair.

Her heart hammered as he pressed her closer, flattening her breasts to the wall of his chest. She wanted to believe she felt like heaven, but she knew for a fact that he felt like temptation, trouble and sin. And he made her want all of the above.

He nuzzled her forehead with his lips and scattered nibbling kisses on her cheek, jaw and a lovely little spot just beneath her earlobe that made her gasp.

"Ah," he said, his voice rife with male satisfaction.

Ah, indeed. Score one for his side. But she couldn't quite find the will to care that he'd found a vulnerable place. It felt too good. It had been too long. And when was he going to get to her mouth? she wondered.

When his lips captured hers, she couldn't manage to stifle her own small sigh of satisfaction. His mouth was soft yet firm, although that didn't make a whole lot of sense. But nothing about this whole thing did. He kissed her slowly, taking his time with tiny nibbling caresses. He could keep that up forever, she thought as tension coiled low in her belly. Heat flared over her skin. She was like fuel just waiting for the spark that would make her go up in flames.

Kamal traced her top lip with his tongue, then went to work on the bottom one, a move that stepped up her heart rate by a lot. When she opened her mouth, he didn't hesitate to dip inside, and the simple motion was like touching a match to kerosene. That single movement, mimicking the act of making love, filled her with yearning. Suddenly she couldn't get close enough or touch him hard enough.

He tunneled his long fingers into her hair and pressed his hand to the back of her head, making the contact of their mouths more firm. She could hear his ragged breathing and felt the desire that built within him yearning for release.

Finally, he dropped a kiss first on her forehead, then her cheek just before he drew in a deep breath and gently removed her arms from around his neck. He pressed his lips to her palm and folded her fingers over it before dropping her hand. Taking one step back, he ran his fingers through his hair. She felt adrift on a sea of emotion without an anchor. And she missed his warmth.

He stared at her, boldly assessing her though his own breathing was none too steady. Say something, she thought. She could be glib if he gave her something to work with. But he simply waited.

"That's one heck of a negotiating technique you've got going there," she finally managed to say. The words were hardly more than a husky whisper and she'd so wanted cool, calm and in control.

"I am waiting to hear you say yes."

There was an edge to his voice telling her she wasn't the only one who'd felt the earth move. Darn it. If she'd heard indifference or his own brand of sexy arrogance, she'd have been able to say gosh darn, you and me is not a good idea. Thanks, but no thanks. Instead, sparks arced between them, feelings she didn't want, need or understand. How could she make a decision under these circumstances?

"I—I'll have to get back to you on this." She swallowed hard. "I need to go check on Johara. Good night, Kamal," she said and turned away.

As she hurried away from him, thoughts tumbled through her mind almost as fast as her feet moved. She could have been less smooth, but she wasn't sure how. All she could hope was that her exit didn't look too much like the flat-out running away it was.

She thought she'd been prepared. The first time he'd kissed her, she'd been engaged to be engaged and he'd taken her by surprise, which was why he'd left her wanting more. This time, he'd actually warned her. And she still wanted more.

None of this made her feel any better about being right that he would be a featured player in her foreign adventure. After Turner proposed to a rich socialite, Ali had felt used—and sad for the wasted time. But she'd never expected another man who didn't even pretend to love her would blatantly ask her to have an affair with him. At least the crown prince was up front about his intentions. He wasn't faking emotions he didn't feel to get what he wanted from her. And she was a sophisticated woman who no longer had stars in her eyes. All of that should have made her decision easier.

It didn't.

He'd called her bluff. So much for straightforward stalling. A flush crept over her skin as she recalled his

request, boldly issued without flourish or ambiguity.
Well, she would just see his direct approach and raise
him a retreat or two.

Kamal left the meeting of the hospital board of directors and thought of Ali. Not a particularly new experience. The comely American had been on his mind
often. Four days ago in the palace garden, he'd made
known to her that she was his choice for an affair.
Though she lived in the palace, he hadn't seen her
since. Yet she'd become even more of a distraction,
making it a challenge to concentrate on business.

Her abrupt departure from the garden that night had
intrigued him. In his experience, women did not "get
back to him." They were only too eager to accommodate his wishes. He had decided to bide his time
and let her mull over his proposition. Lulling your
quarry into a false sense of security to keep them off
guard was another effective negotiating technique. After kissing her, that was his bargaining style of choice.

But it was imperative that he put Ali in her place
and get her off his mind. The time had come for him
to take aggressive action. In his considerable experience with women, familiarity bred boredom. The best
way to get her out of his system was to get on with
the affair. After short duration, he would end it and
choose a wife.

But first things first. After making inquiries, he'd
been told she was conducting orientation for new staff
members in the continuing-education room. It was at
the end of the hall on this very floor. He was looking
forward to seeing Ali in action. And he didn't just
mean as a nurse.

He quietly let himself into the room containing several long, narrow tables surrounded by gray plastic

chairs. Ali stood at the front behind a lectern. Five young women raptly listened to her every word. Soundlessly, he pulled out a chair in the rear and sat. But he knew she'd seen him when the pulse at the base of her throat began to flutter wildly. The proof that she was affected by his presence was most satisfying and information he would put to excellent use in his own good time.

He was vaguely puzzled by what it was about this particular woman that made him so determined to achieve his goal. She was lovely and desirable, as he'd already told her. Even in this windowless room, with overhead fluorescent lights that didn't normally enhance eye color and skin tone, her visual appeal was undiminished. But he'd met and had affairs with numerous beautiful women who did not hold his interest. All were eminently forgettable. What was it about Ali that made her so hard to banish from his thoughts? Surely it was because, as yet, he'd failed to coax from her an affirmative answer to his offer. Soon, he thought.

"That's pretty much it, ladies," Ali said as she rifled through her notes at the lectern. "You've had the grand tour and I've outlined hospital procedures, employee rights, privileges and benefits. Are there any questions?"

He raised his hand when none of her new nurses did.

"Ladies, we have a visitor. May I present His Royal Highness, Kamal Hassan. He is the primary reason we are all here. We have him to thank for this fabulous facility."

"Ladies." He smiled when everyone turned to look at him.

"You had a question, Your Highness?" Ali asked.

"May I have a word with you when you are finished orienting your staff?"

"Of course."

Her tone was professional, cool almost. But he would wager she had no idea how very sensuous her voice was, how the timbre stroked his nerve endings, pleasing him at the same time increasing his eagerness to have her.

"Ladies," she said, "I want to leave you with one last thought. As nurses we are charged to do no harm, but that's not as easy as it sounds. Most of us became nurses because we want to help people. It's a proactive profession and we're eager to fix others. But sometimes it's prudent to stand back and observe, don't jump the gun. Remember, do no harm. Sometimes we serve best when we watch and wait."

As he'd been doing with her, Kamal thought. He could only hope his waiting had increased her anticipation, predisposing her to acquiescence. There was a flurry of activity in the room. The hospital's newest employees gathered papers into their employment packets and filed out of the room, giving him curious looks as they passed.

When he was alone with Ali, he stood and walked to the front of the room. "Ali."

"Kamal," she said.

"You are well?" he asked.

She looked even more lovely now that he was closer to her. Even in her hospital attire—green scrubs and white lab coat with her name and title embroidered on the breast—she stirred his blood.

"I'm fine."

"You have not taken meals in the palace with the

family," he said, unable to keep the faintly disapproving tone from his voice.

"Since your sister refuses to see her father, I thought it more important to keep her company at breakfast and dinner."

"I see. Your devotion to Johara is commendable."

"Her due date is just a couple weeks away. It's my goal to keep her as healthy as possible in body and spirit."

"So you were not avoiding me?" he asked.

"No," she answered too quickly.

"Your only motivation in taking meals with Johara is to do no harm?"

She smiled. "I didn't think you were listening."

"You were wrong."

She drummed her fingers nervously on the wooden lectern beside her. "Was there something you wanted?"

You, he thought. But this was not the time to say so.

"Yes. There is another matter."

The pulse in her throat fluttered briskly once again. She was thinking about their affair. As was he. But it was best to keep your quarry off guard.

"What is it?"

"I am forming a Quality Council to be the organizational and troubleshooting arm of the hospital board of directors."

"I see." The small breath she released could be relief.

"All levels of employees will be represented–housekeeping staff, patient-care personnel, managers all the way to administration."

"How can I help?"

"I wish you to be one of the managers represented."

"Is this committee just for show?"

He knew what she was asking and shook his head. "You will have the opportunity to alter and improve hospital policy as the need arises."

"A governing branch with bite," she said absently.

"Just so," he agreed. "I will give you a chance to think it over. You can get back to me with your answer."

Her gaze lifted to his and the gold in her hazel eyes darkened, making the green more green. He'd deliberately paraphrased the response she'd made to him just before fleeing the garden.

"I can give you an answer now. I relish the opportunity to make a difference in the hospital. At the same time, it will be a good way to enhance my résumé."

He nodded. "Very well. I will inform you when the first meeting will take place."

"I'll look forward to it."

"As will I."

She blinked. "You're going to be there?"

"Of course. I wish to assure myself that this facility is the finest of its kind in the region. Is that a problem?"

"Not at all," she said quickly. "Your devotion is commendable."

"I am a very devoted man when I set my sights on a goal," he said pointedly.

She caught her full bottom lip between her teeth as she studied him. "Speaking of goals," she said.

"Yes?"

"I've noticed a great deal of increased activity in the hospital in the last few days. Would you care to tell me what's going on?"

He folded his arms over his chest. He'd been so sure she was going to give him an answer to the question burning through him. He'd been wrong. She was quite a worthy quarry, he thought as his admiration for her increased.

"As I'm sure you are aware, the hospital is open and accepting patients."

"Yes."

"I wish to have a formal, official opening. Preparations are in progress for the gala to dedicate the hospital. It will also raise funds for research."

"That's always a good thing. Health care doesn't come cheap—even in El Zafir where money is no object."

"It's always significant, especially to those of my people who don't have it. But my objective is to provide a focus for advancing technology and the most up-to-date medical research for my people. It will take brilliant minds and the expertise of practitioners from all over the world. Breakthroughs will, of course, be shared with the rest of the global medical community."

"Do you have a plan for this medical think tank?"

"Yes. In conjunction with the gala, we are going to host a medical symposium. Physicians primarily from the United States, but also specialists from all over the world have been invited to attend and share ideas."

"What a wonderful opportunity."

"It is my intention to make this an annual event. The world community must pull together not only politically, but medically in order to find a cure for cancer and heart disease. There is still a need to eradicate childhood illness, infant mortality and complications of birth."

"That's terrific," she said, smiling up at him as if he had single-handedly saved the world.

He savored the expression in her eyes. "For this first symposium, I have chosen to be selfish. Most of the topics proposed pertain to the smooth and efficient running of a medical facility."

"Since this one is just up and running, it's a good idea to implement sound policy right from the beginning," she commented. "Speaking of that, something I would like to bring up at the first Quality Council meeting is a philosophy that's catching on in the States. Have you heard of the 'no blame' policy?"

He shook his head. "Explain."

"It's a method to reduce or eliminate mistakes in the long run."

"I do not understand. When a mistake is made, the person responsible should feel the weight of consequences."

"That's just it," she said. "We're taught that when we make a mistake there will indeed be consequences. That makes the average employee reluctant to own up to an error. It's why teens lie to their parents—to avoid being grounded. And the primary reason, specifically in a hospital, why workers attempt to cover up their mistakes."

"So what is this policy of which you speak?"

"The theory is to encourage employees to come forward without fear of consequences. Sometimes there may be a breakdown in the system and not the individual. So instead of sweeping a problem under the rug, it can be identified, dealt with and avoided in the future."

"Interesting."

"Knowledge of an existing problem should generate education, not discipline."

He shook his head. "It is a difficult concept. In my experience, if one does something wrong, punishment should follow. With the intention of instilling a need to avoid mistakes in the future."

It was his reason for constructing this facility. To right a wrong and avoid loss of life.

"Are you all right?" she asked, studying him intently. "You have the strangest look on your face."

"I am fine, merely contemplating your theory. I do not think it will work."

"But don't you see? It makes perfect sense. If employees can come forward without fear of losing their jobs, day-to-day functioning is far more efficient. That's a win for the patients who receive better care."

"The possibilities are most interesting," he said.

But not as intriguing as the way her eyes glowed when she warmed to the topic of conversation. Or the manner in which her mouth curved up at the outside. Or the effort of will he exerted to keep himself from kissing her again. He wished to be the topic she warmed to. Which was the very reason he must leave.

He'd accomplished what he came to do. She was reminded of his proposition and would expect him to press for an answer.

"Yes, they are interesting. And if you've got a few minutes, we can talk—"

He shook his head. "I am late for a business meeting in the palace."

"Oh."

It pleased him that she seemed somewhat deflated at his answer. "I must go now. Have a nice day, Ali."

"You, too. Bye, Kamal."

He walked out the door without looking back. He didn't trust himself not to take her in his arms and give in to the temptation to kiss her again. But doing so would spoil his plan for tonight.

Chapter Five

Ali relaxed into the cushy, camel-colored leather of the royal limousine for the short ride back to the palace. Kamal had insisted the car and driver be at her disposal for the daily trip to and from the hospital. The luxury wasn't hard to take. It almost made her forget the unsettling conversation she'd had earlier with Mr. Tall, Dark and Mysterious.

He'd made more than one comment she knew was meant to remind her that he wanted an answer about an affair. *He was a very devoted man when he set his sights on a goal.* The look in his eyes, as if he could devour her, had told her she was his goal. *The possibilities are most interesting.* She would bet her favorite pair of suture scissors that he hadn't been referring to the ''no blame'' philosophy of management she'd been telling him about. In fact, she could read a seductive subtext into almost everything, except that he'd walked away without a backward glance.

What was that about? Maybe she should be relieved

that he'd lost interest. In her experience it usually took a man longer than four days to turn his back on her, but none of those men had been a prince of the desert. Or should she be annoyed that he hadn't followed through on his proposition? Neither, she thought. Her overriding feeling was deep disappointment as she sighed and watched the scenery of El Zafir's capital city fly by.

The car rode like a hovercraft through the streets, gliding over bumps and dips in the road as if they weren't there. Then it turned into the walled and gated royal complex. The palace, a large, lovely, graceful structure with pink stucco walls, waited at the end of a long driveway bordered by lush plants and trees. Bougainvillea and jasmine vined up the exterior walls that protected the compound. The late-afternoon sun still shone on this beautiful fall day, but it didn't improve her mood.

The limo stopped at the bottom of a stone stairway leading to the palace entrance. Ali stepped out, irritated that she couldn't shake her frustration over Kamal. Quickly, she made her way to her room, hoping she wouldn't run into him. The idea made her smile. The palace was so big, without an appointment running into anyone was unlikely.

Inside the suite, she changed quickly into jeans and a T-shirt. She planned to have dinner here with Johara, so dressing up wasn't required. Before she could pick up the phone to dial the princess, there was a knock on her door.

When she opened it, she recognized Emir, Kamal's personal assistant.

"Good afternoon, Miss Matlock," he said.

"Hello."

"I have been instructed by the crown prince to take you to him."

Her heart started to pound. Silly, because he probably wanted nothing more than to discuss hospital-related work. Still, it was considerate of him to send an escort since she wasn't all that familiar with the palace yet. But she knew Kamal's office was located in the business wing and she had a general idea where that was.

When they reached the ground floor, Emir led her through the maze, past sitting rooms and down a long, marble-tiled hall. Paintings, tapestries and exquisite crystal sconces lined the walls. When they came to a T-intersection, she knew the business wing was to the left. But Emir had gone right.

"Wait," she called. "The crown prince's office is this way."

The slender, dark-eyed young man smiled. "Yes. But that is not where the crown prince waits. If you will please follow me?"

"Okay." Her curiosity cranked up a notch.

Anticipation hummed through her and a sense of excitement tiptoed over her skin. They meandered through the back half of the palace and out a rear entrance, down more steps to a path. She followed her guide to the parking garage where the royal fleet of expensive cars had their very own house. A Mercedes SUV was parked at the entrance to the structure. Arms folded over his chest, Kamal leaned against the car waiting.

He was dressed in what she'd learned was the traditional clothing of his country—loose-fitting, white cotton trousers with a matching long-sleeved shirt that opened in a V at his collarbone. Several dark, curling chest hairs peeked out of the gap. A bright, royal-blue sash was tied around his waist, giving him the look of a desert pirate. Though she tried to act as if this sort of thing happened to her every day, Ali knew that one listen with a run-of-the-mill stethoscope would betray her runaway heart.

The young man bowed deferentially. "Miss Matlock, Your Highness."

"Well done, Emir. You may go. Enjoy your evening," Kamal said.

"Thank you, Your Highness. And may you enjoy yours as well."

Ali heard the departing footsteps fade, but couldn't look away from Kamal's mesmerizing gaze. "What's going on?"

"I wish you to join me for dinner this evening."

She looked down at her oldest, most comfortable jeans. "I'm not dressed for it."

"Your attire is completely appropriate for where we're going."

"And where would that be?"

"You'll see." He opened the passenger door. "If you will get in?"

Should she? The moment she'd been told he'd sent for her, and the instant she'd seen him waiting, her down-in-the-dumps mood had evaporated. That should be a warning. But this scenario had adventure written all over it. That was tempting enough, but what tipped the scales was the realization that he hadn't forgotten about her.

"Dinner would be great," she said, stepping past him. "But what about Johara? She won't know where I am."

"She has been informed that you will be with me.

And where we are going communication is excellent. She can easily be in touch should the need arise.''

He'd certainly been sure of himself. But her spirits were too high to be annoyed. "Okay."

She grabbed the handhold and put a foot on the running board. Kamal took her elbow and assisted her into the car and her skin tingled where his strong fingers touched.

When she was settled, he went around to the other door and got in. She looked at him. "No driver?"

"I wish to be in the driver's seat." He met her gaze, then put on aviator sunglasses that hid his eyes. "My security staff will follow us and establish a safe but discreet perimeter."

"I see. Just a guy having dinner with a woman?"

He turned the key in the ignition and the car purred to life. "Just so."

"Yeah, like I believe that."

"Every man needs to eat and an attractive dining companion is most desirable."

"Look, Kamal, I want a regular, ordinary man as much as the next woman, but—"

"You *want* an ordinary man?"

"Sure." She shrugged. "After Turner I learned what's important. A guy who goes to work in the morning and comes home at night to me and our 2.4 children. An honest, hardworking, down-to-earth, average guy who puts his family first and his pants on one leg at a time."

"There is no other way one can put pants on." He glanced at her, frown lines visible over the top of his sunglasses. "It is another American expression stating the obvious."

"Yeah, I guess we like to do that," she agreed.

He eased the car out of the compound, then followed the road to a turnoff that led into the desert. Soon there was nothing around them but windswept sand dunes as far as the eye could see.

While she waited for him to speak, Ali stole glances at his profile and wondered if it was his good side. Then she couldn't help thinking he probably didn't have a bad side. His jawline was strong, with a square chin that hinted at stubbornness. When she glanced out the window again, there was still nothing but desert. Where in the world was he taking her?

"So, tell me about this restaurant we're going to," she said.

"It is not a restaurant."

Right. That would be too average for a man like him. "So we're going to a barbecue?"

He glanced at her and the corners of his mouth turned up in a mysterious smile. "No."

She'd wanted mystery and adventure. File this under the heading Be Careful What You Wish For.

"Okay. Let me guess. You're turning me over to white slavers at an oasis in the desert." When he glanced at her, she noted a brief flash of his white teeth. How nice that she could amuse him.

"You're half-right," he said.

"Which half?"

"You will have to wait and see."

Irritating man, she thought, folding her arms over her chest. "How much longer till we get there?"

"Not long."

Obviously he wasn't going to give her much information so she sat back and enjoyed the ride. It wasn't the limousine, but still pretty luxurious wheels that would no doubt spoil her for anything she could afford back home.

After driving for about an hour, they topped a dune where she found out the half of her ''white slaver'' remark she'd been right about was an oasis. She blinked several times to make sure she wasn't hallucinating. It was the most amazing thing. Stretched below them in the middle of the desert were probably several acres of land where palm trees and plants surrounded a large tent. A crystal-clear stream flowed into a small lake.

He pulled up in front of the tent and turned off the engine. ''We are there now.''

''What is this place?''

''It is where my father, brothers and I come for personal reflection.''

So that's what the royal family was calling seduction these days. ''Sort of home away from home?''

''Just so. Would you like the tour?''

''Absolutely.''

After they exited the SUV, he took her elbow and escorted her inside. When her eyes adjusted after the brightness outside, she saw that the interior was sectioned off into rooms. Kamal showed her the living areas, bedrooms and everything in between. The floor was covered with thick, fringed rugs that she guessed were Persian. And no doubt expensive. On the walls, tapestries and sconces made one forget that this was, in fact, a tent. It might be home away from home, but it was definitely up to royal palace standards.

Kamal led her to the dining area, which was dominated by a heavily carved cherry-wood table set for two with fragile crystal, delicate china and goldware. No plastic forks and paper plates at this barbecue. Flowers

were arranged throughout the room and she breathed
deeply of the fresh floral scent. Although she knew all
he'd had to do was pick up a phone to arrange this,
she was still impressed by the royal treatment. All the
fire retardant in the world couldn't extinguish the glow
inside her.

A uniformed server appeared with a silver tray bearing two flutes holding what she guessed was champagne. Taking one, she said, "Thank you."

Kamal took the other. "To what shall we drink?"

"To ordinary."

One of his dark eyebrows lifted, but he merely
touched the rim of his glass to hers. If she'd had any
doubts about it being genuine crystal, the gentle musical *ping* dispelled them.

The white-jacketed server appeared again. "Your
Highness, would you care to have dinner served now?"

When Kamal looked at her, Ali nodded. "I'm starv-
ing."

"We will eat now," he said.

He held out a chair that sat at a right angle to the
one at the head of the table. Ali sat, and placed the fine
linen napkin in her lap. Kamal took his place and instantly attendants arrived with salads and linen-
wrapped bread in a silver basket. They ate each course
of an exquisitely prepared dinner that would rival the
quality of any world-class restaurant. Some barbecue,
she thought.

When the server appeared and quietly asked what
else they required, Kamal dismissed him and his staff
for the rest of the evening. Until now, Ali had been on
opulence overload. She'd been challenged to keep up
with each successive surprise. But now they were alone
and she remembered that he'd asked her to have an

affair. This intimate dinner was his "ordinary" way to pump up the volume on the offer.

And it was working. But all the champagne and delicacies in the kingdom couldn't make her admit that to him. It didn't matter where she saw him—palace, hospital, oasis—she was drawn to his charm and intelligence like ants to picnic potato salad. As she toyed with the gold fork resting on her china dessert plate, she was grateful for the obvious trappings of affluence. Everything in the tent said he was a prince and she was a pauper.

The whole environment would help keep her head on straight. She would never fit in his world and he wasn't what she was looking for. If she decided to take this "thing" between them to another level, it would have to be without expectations of forever. Maybe a no-strings fling was just what the doctor ordered. With all the reminders, how could she get hurt?

"Let us retire to somewhere more comfortable."

"I'm perfectly fine right here," she said. In spite of the mental pep talk, she wasn't quite ready to take the step.

"As you wish." But there was a gleam in his dark eyes as he replenished her wine. "What would you like to do?"

"Talk," she said too quickly.

"About what?"

Good question. Something impersonal. Something they both had in common. "I'm curious. Why was it so important to you to build the hospital?"

A frown settled over his features and his mouth compressed to a straight line. For several moments he was quiet and she thought he wasn't going to answer.

"Odd that you should ask that. As you Americans would say, this is the scene of my crime."

"What crime?"

His words had shocked her into the automatic question, but she remembered the strange expression on his face earlier when she was telling him about the "no blame" hospital philosophy. What could he possibly have done?

"I feel some responsibility for the death of my father's second wife."

She couldn't believe what he was telling her. The woman had died from complications of pregnancy. Either he had a flair for the dramatic or an overly developed sense of responsibility. But she stayed quiet, waiting for him to go on.

"I was just home from college. My father was scheduled to attend a meeting of oil countries in the region. Daria was in her seventh month of pregnancy but she wanted to go with him."

"Why didn't she?" Ali gently prodded when he hesitated.

"Her pregnancy with Johara was difficult. She'd been advised not to bear more children, but she was determined to give my father a son. The doctor would not let her fly. She insisted she would be fine and urged my father to go. He would be back in plenty of time for the baby."

"That sounds like standard procedure," she said. "What happened?"

"She missed the king and was feeling restless and cooped up in the palace. The two of them often came to the oasis. It is here that my father renews his strength and spirit through reminders of his ancestry. I suggested Daria clear it with her doctor and come here to get away. And she agreed.''

Ali had a bad feeling about what was coming next. ''Go on.''

''I received a frantic call from her maid. Daria had started bleeding. I dispatched the helicopter with the doctor. Unfortunately the bleeding was too severe. By the time she arrived at the clinic in the city, the blood loss was too great and there was nothing that could be done to save her or the child.''

''But her doctor okayed the trip. How is that your fault?''

His gaze met hers. ''She had not consulted the doctor. And she had started—what is the term?''

''Spotting?''

''Yes. She had started spotting before she left the palace.''

''But you didn't know.''

He shook his head. ''It does not matter what I knew. If I had not suggested the trip, help would have been closer. I vowed to Johara that I would build the finest medical facility money could buy so that other little girls would not suffer the same pain as she had to. But that was small comfort to a five-year-old child who was bereft at the loss of her mother. She took to following me around.''

''Why you? Why not her father?''

''She is the image of Daria. The king could not bear to look at his daughter.''

That explained a lot, she thought. ''I'm sorry your family went through such a tragedy.''

He met her gaze and his own simmered with emotion. ''But?''

She decided not to ask him how he knew there was

a but. "Obviously you've been carrying around this guilt like a security blanket."

"What does that mean?"

"Today when we were talking about hospital policy, you said if one does something wrong, punishment should follow. I'm not sure why you feel the need to take the blame for Daria's death. You did nothing wrong."

"Then why does it feel that way?"

"Because it was a lousy thing that happened. But you didn't make it so, Kamal. You're not all-powerful. You suggested something you thought would bring her comfort. She could have refused to go. Even if she'd stayed in the palace, if the bleeding was severe enough, it's quite possible she still couldn't have been saved. It's been twelve years. Let it go."

He sipped his wine, then set his stemmed glass on the table. "Is that an order?"

"Now that you mention it—" She looked at him. "It occurs to me, what took you so long to make good on that vow to build the hospital?"

One corner of his mouth curved up. "The planning stage was long and painstaking. It was necessary to lay a foundation for a health-care system in this country before work on the actual construction could begin. My country was waging financial battles on many fronts to bring us in line with Western culture. Convincing the right people to allocate the necessary funds took time."

"And now it's done."

"Yes." Pride echoed in his voice.

"Your penance is done, your vow is kept. Isn't it time to forgive yourself and let go of the past?"

"That is easier said than done. When I see my sister with child, I can't help wondering if she would be facing such a thing had her mother lived to guide her through the rebellious years.''

Ali could see the pain and guilt still swirling in his dark eyes. And something else, too.

"You love your sister very much, don't you?''

"'Yes,'' he answered simply.

Everything he'd done proved it. "So, let me get this straight. It's all right to love your family? But it's not okay to be 'in love' with one woman?''

"Just so. I am pleased that you have a rational grasp of the concept.''

He couldn't be more wrong. She shook her head. "Love is an involuntary reaction to specific stimuli, which is different for every person on the planet. Some people call it chemistry. Some say it's pheromones. Whatever the mysterious criteria is that attracts one person to another leading to deeper emotion is irrelevant. You can't control such a feeling.''

He straightened in his chair as he met her gaze. "I am Kamal Hassan, crown prince and heir to the throne of El Zafir. Of course I can exert power over such things.''

"Okay.''

"You sound skeptical,'' he said. "Why?''

"Because you're a man.''

"That is so. But I still do not understand.''

"My skepticism about love and relationships might have something to do with the way my father treated my mother. He divorced her because he found someone better—a woman with money and connections to put his struggling construction company on the map. It was so painful and humiliating for my mother, she moved the two of us away. After that, I rarely saw my father. He couldn't be bothered with anything as mundane as visitations with me. But he seemed to love his second wife. Last I heard, they were still together. And he had two other daughters to take my place.''

"A man who would abandon his child is a jackal.'' His voice shook with anger.

"Your father abandoned your sister,'' she said.

"He allows her shelter under his roof. For his generation, it is the best he can do.''

His clipped tone warned her not to point out that it was still emotional abandonment. "If you say so.''

"Family affection and responsibilities are a sacred trust that can never be broken. Your father is a poor excuse for a man and his actions prove that I am right to avoid romantic love. It makes a man weak.''

He was right about her father, but she'd always figured the man had a defect of character. And Turner—same thing. But Kamal assumed the burdens of his country—his people. Maybe it was expected of the man who would be king. Or maybe he was a perfectionist. But he was stronger than any man she'd ever met, with the moral backbone that went along with it.

He really believed what he was saying. She sighed. If these hoity-toity surroundings didn't help keep her head on straight, his words convinced her. It was okay to be attracted to Kamal as long as she remembered there was no future in loving him. He would marry and produce an heir because it was his duty and to do less was weak. But duty was all it would ever be because he wouldn't let himself love any woman and risk being less than his best as king.

"Romantic love is something I want,'' she told him, standing. "And I intend to find it someday with an ordinary guy who's looking for the same things out of life I am.''

He stood up and held out his hand. "Come here."

For the life of her she didn't know why, but she put her fingers in his palm and let him draw her close to his body. She could feel the heat of his skin, smell the spicy fragrance of his cologne, see that he had no five-o'clock shadow, meaning he'd shaved for her. He put her hand on his chest and encircled her waist with his arm, snuggling her close.

"We have wasted far too much time discussing serious matters. Now I wish to kiss you."

Even if he hadn't told her, the smoldering look in his eyes let her know that he intended to put his mouth where it would be most effective in negotiating an affirmative answer from her. With every fiber of her being she wanted to say yes. Sweep me away. When his lips settled on hers, her eyelids drifted closed as she savored the heat of his hard, lean body.

He was deepening the kiss, when the strident ringing of his cell phone startled her. He lifted his head and annoyance was written all over his face. She would hate to be the person on the other end of the call. It had better be important, she thought, trying to control her breathing.

He flipped the phone open. "Yes?" he growled into the receiver.

As he listened, annoyance vanished and was replaced by a completely different emotion. If she had to guess, she would call it fear.

"Send the helicopter for me immediately." He snapped the phone closed.

"What is it?"

"My sister's labor has begun. It is too early."

Chapter Six

Ali took his big hands in hers and squeezed. "It's not like before. This is nothing like what happened with her mother."

"It is too early," he said again.

"Only a couple of weeks. Besides, determining a due date isn't an exact science. And first babies are notoriously unpredictable."

"Dammit, where is the helicopter?" he said, pulling his hands from hers. He started pacing like a caged tiger. "Fate is a harsh mistress. How ironic that I should be here when her time comes."

"If anyone should feel guilty, it's me. Johara specifically asked me to be with her because she was nervous. And where am I?"

"It is because *I* spirited you away," he said, tapping his chest.

"Kamal, listen to me." She planted herself in his path, forcing him to stop and deal with her. "You can't take responsibility for the whole world. You have to delegate.''

"That is not my way.''

How could you not like this man? Ali thought. He had an infinite capacity to care for everyone else. And he was something of an overachiever—at the expense of his own personal happiness.

He started to go around her to pace and she stepped to the side, again blocking him as she put a hand on his chest. He was tall, strong and could bulldoze her in a heartbeat if he chose. But she couldn't imagine him hurting anyone. And she was determined that he would listen to the rest she had to say.

"Thanks to you, Johara is five minutes away from the finest facility money can buy with the most up-to-date technology. Her doctor is there. He's one of the best I've ever worked with.''

"It's not enough.''

"She's going to be fine. She's probably already at the hospital—with skilled medical personnel around her.''

"I want you with my sister. Where is the damn chopper?''

Ali couldn't remember hearing him swear before. He'd done it twice in the last two minutes. In the distance she heard a rumble indicating the helicopter was close. What a relief. The downside of a man who took responsibility for everything was that he wouldn't be convinced that there were things he couldn't fix. This time there was nothing he could do but wait. This time, it was her job to help.

"And I will be with her soon,'' she said, looking down at her jeans. "Although I'm not dressed for work.''

But she was almost relieved about the interruption. Her clothes were supercasual. And if he'd made the slightest move to separate her from them, she wouldn't have lifted a finger to stop him. She'd been so caught up in his kiss, she couldn't have uttered a word of protest. If his phone hadn't rung when it did…

Saved by the cell.

Unable to sit still, Kamal paced the hospital waiting room. He and Ali had arrived at the facility's heliport on the roof five hours ago. His brothers, their wives and his aunt Farrah were all in the room talking quietly as they sat on the couches and chairs scattered throughout the room. A television was mounted high on the wall and a world-news program was displayed.

Everyone kept telling him there was no reason for alarm. But he couldn't ignore a disturbing feeling of déjà vu. He'd done this before—waited for news of a mother and baby. His anxiety was the same, only the surroundings and the players were different. Would the outcome be the same? He despised this feeling of helplessness.

Fariq stood and stepped into his path. "You will wear out the brand-new carpeting."

"I don't care." He started to move around his middle brother.

"Kamal, you must have faith. Johara will be fine. As will her baby."

"That is easy for you to say. You have two healthy children."

"And I give thanks for that every day. Don't forget, we all lived through the tragedy of our father's beloved wife and the child who would have been our brother.

No one blames you except yourself. But it is unlikely this birth will be anything but normal."

Kamal ran his fingers through his hair. "There are no guarantees."

"That is true." His brother let out a long breath. "We can only wait and see."

Kamal nodded, but Ali's words ran through his mind. He'd done everything humanly possible to make the hospital the finest facility and fill it with the most modern equipment. He had assembled a staff of health-care professionals with the best training available. Johara's doctor had impeccable credentials.

The memory of her words brought him a measure of comfort. He'd availed himself of her support and been far too grateful for her presence when he'd received the news about his sister's labor. The weakness infuriated him.

Fariq placed a reassuring hand on his shoulder. "Believe me, brother, history will not repeat itself."

Kamal nodded, but in his heart he could not believe. History repeated itself all the time. The same mistakes were made over and over. And he was his father's son. What if the fascination he felt for Ali became more? What if he was like his father and could not control it? He'd been trained from boyhood to become king and he wished only to be a good one. He yearned to leave his country a better place for his leadership.

But what if he became weak and could not do his job? Like his father. He could not let that happen. He must continue to struggle against his feelings and not let them become more. Somehow he must find a way to banish Ali from his thoughts along with the hold she'd begun to have on him.

The door opened and Dr. McCullough entered the

room dressed much like Ali—white lab coat over green scrubs. The middle-aged doctor looked tired as he lifted his wire-rimmed glasses and rubbed his eyes. Was it fatigue or defeat?

"Doctor?" Kamal walked over to him and felt the rest of his family behind him although he hadn't heard anyone move. "How is my sister?"

Dr. McCullough smiled. "She has a healthy baby boy. Five and a half pounds."

Kamal smiled and let out a relieved breath as cheers and clapping erupted around him. "And Johara? Is she all right?"

The doctor nodded as he rubbed a hand across his face. "She's tired and sore, which is all normal after giving birth. It's called labor for a reason."

"I can hardly wait," Penny said.

Rafiq draped an arm across her shoulders. "I will not leave your side. If I could go through it for you, I would."

"Easy for you to say." But she rested her blond head against his chest.

"Actually the princess had a relatively short labor," the doctor said. "In general, first babies take their own sweet time getting here."

"Way to put my mind at ease, Doctor," Crystal commented wryly.

Fariq took her hand and placed a soft kiss on her knuckles. "If there was an elixir or procedure that would make your time easier, I would gladly search the world over to find it."

Crystal smiled at him. "I know you're schmoozing me, but how can I not love that?"

Kamal envied his brothers and the women who loved

them. But as the firstborn son, he was destined for a different fate. It did not include the comfort of love.

"I wish to see my sister," he said.

The doctor nodded. "You can see her for a few minutes. But it's late and, as I said, she's tired. She needs to rest. Everyone else can see her and the baby tomorrow."

His aunt took a cell phone from her pocket. "I will inform the king."

"Thank you," Kamal said.

Then his family thanked the doctor and filed out of the waiting room to the limousine he knew was waiting. Kamal walked to the royal family's birthing room. Extensive research had gone into the planning for the space. It was designed for the comfort of the mother-to-be who labored and delivered her baby there. Then it became a hospital room where she stayed while she recuperated, and was monitored to make sure everything was normal before she went home. There was a connecting door into another room where a family member could stay.

Someday Kamal's children would be born here. And their mother— Instantly, a picture of Ali flashed into his mind. As he pushed open the door to the royal suite, he wished he could as easily push away the image of her holding his son.

He walked into the room and his gaze was instantly drawn to Ali. In her arms was a tiny bundle swaddled in a thin blanket and wearing a blue knit hat. She was smiling at the infant with such tenderness, a deep aching emptiness opened like a black hole inside him. How would it feel to be the object of her devotion? he wondered.

"Kamal!" Johara smiled at him.

He went to the electronically adjustable hospital bed where she semi-reclined. She looked radiant.

"Little sister," he said, bending to kiss her cheek. "You are well?"

She nodded. "Did you see my son?"

He shook his head. Ali was right there beside him. The faint fragrance of her perfume lingered over the smell of hospital cleanliness. Tenderly she pressed back the blanket for him to see the red, wrinkled baby.

"Isn't he beautiful?" Ali asked.

Kamal met her gaze. "I do not think it appropriate to use such an adjective to describe a boy."

Johara laughed. "The doctor says he is a fine strong boy. Do you wish to hold him?"

"Yes." He found he wanted to very much.

Ali had abandoned her jeans and T-shirt for lighter-weight scrubs and he felt the slight brush of her breasts as she settled the sleeping infant in the crook of his elbow. Again he felt an ache for something he did not understand.

"Kamal?"

He looked at his sister and the yearning on her face told him what she wanted to know. "The king knows about your son," he said before she could ask.

"Is he here?" she asked, her eyes brimming with hope.

"No."

"It's late and you need your rest," Ali said quickly. "Your father will see you and the baby tomorrow."

Tears filled his sister's eyes. "No. He will not come."

Kamal was angry that his father's stubborn, old-fashioned pride had put his sister in this position. He'd backed himself into a corner, now there was no way for him to save face.

Johara brushed a tear from her cheek. "Practically the last words he spoke to me were that he no longer has a daughter. Now he has no grandson either."

"He'll change his mind. Give him time," Ali protested.

She shook her head. "I know my father. He is stubborn. To go back on his word is a weakness he will not allow. I refuse to subject my son to such a thing. I will not bring him up in a place where he will be treated with shame for a sin not his own."

"What are you going to do?" Ali asked.

"I will ask the king to let me go to the United States," his sister said.

Kamal knew she'd harbored this dream for a long time. He also knew how their father felt about it. "He will not give his permission."

"Then I will go without it," Johara said.

Ali's troubled gaze settled on him. "Johara is right. If your father doesn't change his attitude toward her and the baby, it wouldn't be healthy to bring him up here."

"You heard the king forbid me to interfere."

"I remember. He said you'd always been weak where your sister was concerned. But that's not true. You became the father to her that he refused to be."

Kamal knew he should regret telling her about the past, but somehow he couldn't.

"My brother," Johara said. "You must help me."

"You've got to." Ali gazed at him with complete and absolute trust and confidence brimming in her eyes. "You're the only one who can."

* * *

Ali saw Kamal outside the conference room in the hospital. Interesting that she saw him here more than in the palace. She'd stayed on there when Johara had brought the baby home two weeks ago. Where had the time gone? The teenager had recovered quickly and was back to normal—physically. Emotionally she was feeling the effects of her father's abandonment.

Kamal hadn't yet seen her. He was going over some papers in his hands and hadn't looked up, giving her a chance to study him. If Kamal Hassan had been the course of study, nursing school would have been a snap. His dark head was bent but she could see the curve of his cheekbone, the strong lean line of his jaw, his tall powerful body in the expensive dark suit. She hadn't seen him in the traditional clothing of his country since the night Johara's baby had been born.

Ali was still staying in the palace at the request of Princess Farrah. The older woman had said her niece would appreciate the help and emotional support. But Johara had insisted on caring for her son without help, saying he was her blessed responsibility. How could you not admire that? But so far her father had not acknowledged the birth of his only daughter's child. And Kamal had done nothing to help his sister. She'd been so sure he would, that when he didn't, it was more of a disappointment than she'd expected.

Ali heard a soft *ding* indicating the elevator had arrived at the second floor. She automatically glanced over her shoulder to see who would exit. The doors whispered open revealing King Gamil. She'd never seen the king here in the hospital before.

"Kamal!"

The king walked past her without even seeing her,

apparently focused on his eldest son. And the older man didn't look happy.

Kamal looked up from his papers. "Father."

"What have you done with Johara?" Fury simmered in his voice.

"What makes you think I've done anything?"

"Because she's not at the palace."

"How do you know this? Did you go to see her?"

The king stood up straighter as his shoulders tensed. "Her maid said she is gone."

Ali felt as if she was caught in a shoot-out with nowhere to take cover. The king stood between her and his son, shielding her. She backed away and inched around the corner, but could still clearly hear voices. It wasn't difficult, since the king was shouting.

"Why would you think I would know where she is?"

"Do not treat me like a fool."

"All right. I arranged for my sister and her child to be taken to a place where they will be safe and happy."

"Tell me where she is."

"Johara asked me not to divulge her whereabouts."

"I am her father. You have no right to keep her location a secret from me. I demand that you tell me."

"I made a promise to my sister and I will not break my word."

"Your word?" His tone was rife with derision. "That is more important than an order from the king?"

"In this case—yes. I assured Johara that I would be there for her always."

"How can you do that when she is not here?"

"I have done that which she asked me to do. I've made it possible for her to raise her son in harmony."

"Against her own father's wishes?"

"You have not been her father for many years now."

Kamal spoke the words quietly, but that wasn't why Ali got chills up and down her spine. It had taken great courage to intervene on his sister's behalf, knowing his father would be ticked off. She knew he held his father in high esteem even though he didn't agree with the way the man treated his daughter. But to stand up to him the way he was—to come right out and tell him he hadn't been a father to her in a long time—he stopped short of quoting what Ali had said about him being the father her own had refused to be.

"You are a weak man, Kamal. I have grave doubts about your ability to be a great king." His voice vibrated with anger and hurt.

The next thing she knew, he walked past her and entered the elevator. She let out a relieved breath and peeked around the corner at Kamal. He was standing in the same place, but the expression on his face was dark.

She rounded the corner and walked to him, putting her hand on his arm. She had a feeling he needed the contact, but even if he didn't, she did. "I just want to say he's wrong."

"My father?"

She nodded. "I probably shouldn't have eavesdropped, but I did. So sue me, or whatever the equivalent expression is here in your country."

"And what is he wrong about?"

"You're going to be an awesome king."

With grave intensity he met her gaze. "And how do you know this?"

"You kept your word, even knowing how upset your father was going to be."

"Some would call me an imbecile. I'm not so sure they wouldn't be correct."

"Well, I'm sure." She took a deep breath. "I can't begin to understand what you'll one day face as the leader of your country. But for my money, what you did for Johara was right and just. Although I'm going to miss her and that adorable baby."

"As will I."

"It's apparent that you love her very much. I know how hard it must be to let her go. That makes what you did so eloquent. What more could your people want in their king?"

"It is my greatest wish to be a good king, to make this a strong country that will take a leadership role in the world order. I wish to make a difference, for the better, in the lives of my people. A weak man cannot accomplish such a thing."

She heard the dejection in his voice and sighed. Rich man, poor man, beggar man, thief—it didn't matter. Parents had a powerful impact on their children. Sometimes not in a good way.

"Your father was angry and frustrated. He lashed out because he's hurting. He didn't mean what he said."

"He meant every word." His mouth compressed to a grim line.

"You knew he would be angry. If you believe what he said about you, why did you do it? Why did you arrange for your sister to leave the country?"

"Because it was right. Because Johara asked." He looked at her and his dark eyes glowed as he placed his hand over hers, still resting on his arm. His mouth turned up at the corners. "And because you wished it."

He squeezed her fingers before turning away and entering the conference room.

Ali blinked several times, not quite sure she wasn't dreaming. Or maybe there was something wrong with her hearing. He'd spirited his sister out of the country against his father's wishes because she, Ali, had asked? Her heart beat so hard she thought her ribs would crack.

Pressing her fingertips to the pounding in her temples, she tried to think. Now that Johara and the baby were gone, she wouldn't be needed in the palace any longer. It was time to pack up and get out of Dodge, so to speak. His life was the palace, hers was not—and never would be, could be or should be. She needed to put some distance between herself and Kamal. If only it could be a continent.

He tried to pretend he only had lofty, distant feelings for family, honor, country. But Ali would never be convinced that a man who would go out on a limb for his sister the way he had didn't possess the capacity for hearth and home, in-the-trenches kind of caring. The thought of being the woman he cared about, the one who could capture his heart in a romantic way, the one he would move mountains for, was seductive. It was like a powerful drug.

It was wrong. Because, even if she wanted it more than anything else in the world, she could never be the right woman. And he knew it too, which was why he wanted an affair. If he continued to pursue the idea, she was in big trouble. Because she wasn't sure what she should do. Before, she might have had a chance of keeping her emotions disengaged.

His heroic gesture made that impossible.

Chapter Seven

Ali walked from room to room in her palace suite looking for any personal items she might have left around. After the Quality Council meeting the previous day, she'd informed Princess Farrah that she was moving back to her apartment in the city's American compound. During her shift today, the palace staff had packed up her things.

Satisfied that nothing had been missed, she zipped up her suitcase, then did the same with her cosmetics bag and placed them in the foyer.

There was a knock on the door and she figured it was the driver Princess Farrah had promised to send for her. But when she answered, it was the princess herself. Behind her was a uniformed server with a cart.

"Ali, dear, I just couldn't let you leave without one last afternoon tea."

Ali was in no hurry to return to an empty apartment. The company was most welcome. And an opportunity

to have tea in a palace might never happen again.
"Come in, please."

The princess smiled and entered the foyer. With a
slight motion of her elegant hand, she bade the server
wheel the cart into the suite. He set out china cups and
a matching graceful teapot on the glass-topped coffee
table in the living room. Then there were finger sand-
wiches, fruit and pastries on a delicate three-tiered
crystal plate trimmed in gold. Last but not least, con-
diments and cloth napkins.

"Do you require anything else, Your Highness?"

"No. Thank you, Khalid."

He nodded, then left.

"Ali, I wish to thank you for your assistance to my
niece," the princess said as she sat in the center of the
semicircular, overstuffed sofa. "I do hope it hasn't
been an inconvenience for you to disrupt your life and
stay here."

Ali sat on the end of the couch, at a right angle to
her. "Princess Farrah, I don't mean to be impertinent
or disrespectful, but it would take a special kind of
stupid to feel inconvenienced by living in a palace."
She gazed around the perfectly appointed room with
its French doors that overlooked the Arabian Sea.

The other woman laughed. "I do not think you are
impertinent at all. You are quite delightful. And we
shall miss you. I think Kamal most of all."

"What makes you say that? I hardly see him." But
Ali found it wasn't entirely the elegance and comfort
of the palace that she would miss. It had something to
do with sleeping under the same roof as the crown
prince. And his aunt's comment made her happy. How
she wished it wasn't so.

"I know he quarreled with the king yesterday."

Ali nodded. "Do you think Kamal did the wrong thing? Helping his sister go away—do you think it was wrong?"

The princess poured tea into two cups. After handing one of them to Ali without milk or sweetener, she stirred some sugar into her own. "I will miss my niece terribly," she started. "And her baby—"

Ali was surprised to see tears in her eyes. "I'm sorry, Your Highness, I shouldn't have asked. If you'd rather not talk about this—"

"It's all right. But the thought of not holding the baby we all waited for so long." She sighed. "It makes me sad. But it is a fact that must be faced."

"Couldn't you go to Johara, wherever she is?"

"Kamal will not divulge her whereabouts—not even to me. I have already asked." Her small smile was wry. "It is his sister's wish that her father not find her. She is concerned that he will bring her back."

"Would he?"

"I know you will not understand, but he loves Johara very much. It is quite possible that he would coerce her into coming home."

Ali studied the troubled look on the woman's face. "Wouldn't that please you?"

"Yes and no. I miss them both very much. But I agree with my niece that this is not a positive environment in which to raise a child. Gamil must learn that the old ways are not always the best. They are merely more comfortable. My niece made a mistake. But treating her harshly would make a waste of not just one, but two lives now. I believe she has learned and will be a good mother and a productive person. Wherever she is." The princess smiled. "It pleases me that you were with Kamal when he clashed with his father."

"I wasn't exactly with him. I overheard the conversation."

"Kamal cares very much for his father and covets his good opinion. Gamil's harsh words troubled him deeply. But he told me what you said afterward. And I must say, his spirits seemed much lighter than I would have expected."

"Will their relationship suffer because of this?"

She hoped not. Especially if part of his reason for helping Johara leave the palace had been as he said— because she wished him to.

"They will cool off. Kamal will tell his father he did what he thought was right and meant no disrespect. Gamil will respond that a man can do no more than what he feels is right. And it will be over."

Ali blinked. "As simple as that?"

"Men can sometimes be simpleminded," the princess said with a shrug. "It is a double-edged sword."

Ali laughed, but she had a question just bursting to be asked. She was leaving the palace anyway, so if she was thrown out, it would only happen a bit sooner. "Is Kamal's father the one who taught him that he can't fall in love *and* be a good king?"

The princess sighed and put her cup and saucer on the table. "It wasn't articulated, but that was the message. My brother fell deeply in love twice and both times lost the woman of his heart. His first wife, the mother of my three nephews, died of cancer."

"Kamal told me how Johara's mother died."

The older woman's eyes were bleak. "Daria's death was unexpected. She was quite young and I think that made it harder on Gamil. He fell into a deep depression and for a time found it difficult to perform his duties. Kamal stepped in for him."

"So he learned that to do a good job, to go down in the history books as a good leader, he must never fall in love?"

"Yes," the princess confirmed. "Love is a weakness and the man who inherits the throne of El Zafir cannot succumb to it."

"That's so sad," Ali said. And she didn't just mean the king losing his wife. There were four children impacted by the loss of their mothers. One of them was Kamal and fate had dealt him a double blow.

"I'm afraid my nephew has learned the lesson too well. He's grown up with the burden of knowing that he will someday rule his people and wishes to do the best possible job. He will not permit personal feelings to impede his duty."

"Isn't part of his duty to produce an heir to the throne?" Ali asked.

"Yes."

"And probably a woman with royal connections would make the ideal mother."

Princess Farrah tilted her head, a vaguely assenting gesture. "My brother has asked for my assistance in compiling a list of suitable candidates as a wife for his son."

"That's very—businesslike," she commented.

"Royal succession and continuity of leadership is serious business," the princess explained. "In your country, there is a president and vice president and the line of succession is defined in your Constitution. But we have been a monarchy for hundreds of years and the leadership role is passed from the king to his eldest son. Kamal has a responsibility to marry and produce an heir. He's had every opportunity to choose his own bride and he has not done so. Time grows short."

"But why?" Dumb question. Kamal had already told her he wouldn't fall in love. Why *would* he want to rush into marriage. "He's not old, Your Highness. Doesn't he have plenty of time?"

The woman shook her head. "His father wishes to retire, but he will not do so until Kamal is married and settled."

Ali felt a chill, and certainly not because the climatic environment in the palace was anything less than perfect. This process of choosing a wife for Kamal was callous and soulless. What a relief that her name wouldn't appear on the list. But deep down, she knew that was a lie. There was something going on between her and Kamal. A connection. Chemistry, whatever you wanted to call it. Unfortunately, exploring their feelings would be an exercise in futility, because a woman like her would never get her name on the wife list.

The princess stood. "I must go. But I wanted you to know how much we appreciate your support of Johara."

Ali stood, too. "It wasn't anything. I just slept here. Kamal was the one who really helped her."

"This isn't goodbye." The other woman walked to the door and opened it. "I'm sure I will see you at the festivities planned for the hospital's official opening."

"I'm sure."

She started to leave, then turned back. "By the way. The physicians invited to the medical symposium are beginning to arrive. I believe one of them comes from the facility where you worked in Texas. Perhaps you know him. Dr. Turner Stevens?"

"Yes." Although her heart had begun to pound, Ali struggled not to react.

''How nice you will see a friend from home. Good-bye, dear.''

''Goodbye.''

Ali closed the door, pleased she'd managed to keep the princess from knowing that her heart was pounding. Know him? You could say that. It was a small world and getting smaller all the time. Of all the oil-rich countries in all the world, he had to show up in hers. She so didn't want to see him. Why else would she have left her old job and traveled halfway around the world?

Ali took her place at the door to the hospital cafeteria. The morning workshops and tour of the facility had just ended and she'd volunteered to answer any questions and direct the visiting physicians to lunch. The royal family's very own chef was doing the honors today and the tables in the large room were set like a five-star restaurant with china, crystal, flowers and candles. No expense had been spared and no detail overlooked in welcoming the doctors to El Zafir's first medical symposium.

She saw tall and tan and young and hunky blond Turner Stevens walk out of the elevator. His long-legged stride brought him quickly down the hall toward her. To go into lunch, he had to pass by her and that was the way she'd planned it.

He stopped in front of her and smiled his movie-star smile. ''Hello, Ali.''

''Turner.'' She put all the friendly she could into her responding smile. ''How are you?''

''Good. What about you?''

What about her? The last time she'd talked to him in Texas, he'd broken the shocking news that he'd proposed to the daughter of the hospital's chief of staff. Stunned didn't begin to describe her feelings that day. She couldn't remember what she'd said. But she vividly recalled that she'd walked away before he could see the tears in her eyes. Before he could tell how hurt and humiliated she was that he'd picked someone better—just as her father had done to her mother. How was she now?

"I'm terrific," she said. "Couldn't be better."

That was stretching it a bit, given her tug-of-war with the crown prince. But Turner didn't need to know about that.

"You look terrific," he responded. "I guess working on the other side of the world agrees with you."

"I guess. Have you had an opportunity to see any of the country?"

"A little."

"It's fabulous. There's a museum near the government buildings downtown that's wonderful. I know how you like museums, and this one depicts pretty comprehensively the history of El Zafir and its people. How oil was discovered, and impacted the economy. I think you'd enjoy it."

"Thanks. I'll do that."

They stared at each other for several awkward moments. He hadn't changed a bit. His eyes were still blue and insincere. He looked as athletic and fit as always. His sandy hair was short and neat.

"I'm surprised—"

"You really should—"

"You go," she said.

"Okay," he agreed. "Dr. McCullough said you volunteered to show us around the hospital this morning. I was a little surprised."

"Because of our past history?"

"Frankly—yes."

She'd done it deliberately. She was in charge of Labor and Delivery and quite a few of the physicians at the conference practiced the specialty. It would have looked strange if she'd chosen that particular time to take a few days off. Under those circumstances, she was bound to run into him and she wanted to do it on her terms. This was her turf, so to speak. She wasn't about to let their first face-to-face meeting in a long time go to chance. She would be prepared and in control and not give him the satisfaction of thinking she was still carrying a torch for him.

She took a deep breath. "You and I are ancient history. This is where I work and I'm very proud of it. This facility is probably the finest, most technologically advanced place I've ever worked. Crown Prince Kamal Hassan has spared no expense to make it that way. This symposium is one of the ways he plans to keep abreast of all the latest advances and breakthroughs in medical technology, procedures and drug research. He plans to make this an annual event."

Turner smiled but it didn't reach his eyes. "He sounds like quite a guy."

"He is."

"Thank you." Kamal walked up behind her.

"I didn't see you," she said, looking up at him beside her.

"You are obviously busy. Please introduce me to your friend."

"Oh, we're not friends," she said automatically. "We used to be—"

"Yes?" he asked, one black eyebrow going up.

She had the feeling he already knew. "Turner Ste-

vens, this is His Royal Highness Kamal Hassan, Crown
Prince of El Zafir and your host for these festivities.''

Turner held out his hand. ''It's a pleasure to meet
you.''

''The pleasure is mine,'' Kamal said. ''Welcome to
my country.''

''Thank you. I'm quite impressed with the hospital.
And the staff,'' he said, glancing at Ali. ''I can tell you
from personal experience that Ali knows her stuff.''

''As can I.'' Kamal's eyes narrowed on the other
man, but his royal smile never wavered. ''There was a
recent addition to the royal family and Ali was of great
assistance.''

The two men made small talk and Ali felt as if she
was watching a competitive tennis match. Could two
men be more different? she wondered. There had been
a time when she'd thought the sun rose and set on
Turner. He was better-looking than the average bear,
intelligent, and an ambitious doctor. She hadn't realized how ambitious until she'd been blindsided by his
proposal to a woman who would be more useful to his
career.

Kamal was dark-eyed and his thick black hair was
wavy, just teasing and tempting a woman to run her
fingers through it. He was also intelligent, handsome
and industrious. He hadn't yet chosen a woman who
would be useful to him in his work, but he would.
However, his motives weren't about himself. In fact,
he was basically sacrificing his personal happiness for
his country and his people.

Once she'd thought Turner was everything she could
hope for in a man—someone who yearned for love and
family, a man who cared about the welfare of others.
As she compared the two men, she found Turner lack-

ing. His hair was lighter than she remembered and the streaks weren't from the sun but an expensive weave at a salon.

He was more interested in his career than a family. Kamal cared about his people, but was so concerned about doing his best that he wouldn't permit himself to fall in love. Distance had given her the perspective to see that what she wanted was just a regular guy who was looking for the same things out of life that she was.

Glancing between the two, she realized neither was an especially good bet. Although she found that tall, dark and handsome made her wish, just for a moment, that Kamal wasn't quite so dedicated.

"Dr. Stevens, I do not wish to make you miss lunch. You have my assurance that it will be most enjoyable."

"I have no doubt, Your Highness." He looked at her. "Ali, will you join me?"

She shook her head. "I have things to do to get ready for this afternoon and tomorrow."

"About that," Kamal said. "I wish to see you regarding the dedication ceremony."

"All right. When?"

"I will send my car for you later, when you have completed work for the day."

She wanted to tell him they should conduct business during regular office hours. Not in the evening. It was too personal. But with Turner standing there and listening to every word, she couldn't. The crown prince of an oil-rich up-and-coming country valued her opinion. She wanted to look Turner in the eye and say *How do you like me now?* And she wished she could tell Kamal her off-hours were her own and she didn't want to spend them with him. But that would be a big fat lie.

So maybe she had something to thank Turner for after all. Because of his presence, she wasn't going to cut off her nose to spite her face.

"Very well, Your Highness. I'll see you later."

"I will look forward to it."

Chapter Eight

Kamal paced the length of his suite, impatient for Ali's arrival. He had dispatched the limousine for her forty-five minutes ago. Her apartment was not that far from the palace. Just as he picked up the phone to make a call, there was a knock on the door and he moved to open it. She stood in the hall. Only years of practice in controlling his emotions prevented him from betraying his eagerness to see her.

"I have been waiting."

"I'm sorry to be so long," she said, walking past him into the foyer.

"The drive from the palace and back does not take so much time."

"No. I left work late and had to freshen up. You weren't worried about me, were you?"

"Of course not," he scoffed. It was almost the truth. "The effort you made was well worth the wait. You look lovely."

She wore a white knit dress and matching jacket that

covered her from neck to ankles. The soft material tantalized at the same time that it concealed, clinging to each of her tempting curves. Her hair was charmingly arranged in a casual style that made him think of running his fingers through it as their bare bodies molded together in a tangle of arms and legs. That picture made the blood flow faster and hotter through his veins.

She smiled at his compliment. "You're just being kind because I know I look like something the cat yakked up. I've been running all day at work. The entire staff in Labor and Delivery was stretched to the limit because several women went into labor at the same time. It seems their babies were unable to wait for the hospital's official opening. All normal deliveries—except one. She had complications."

Gently Kamal nudged her chin up with his knuckle so that he could see into her eyes, study her by the light from the chandelier in the foyer. Purple smudges stained the area just above her sculpted cheekbones, attesting to her fatigue. She was always so strong, eager and ready to help when asked. But who did *she* turn to?

He took her hand and placed it in the bend of his elbow. "Come. I will pour you a glass of wine."

"That's the best offer I've had all day."

He led her into the living room and settled her on the sofa facing the French doors, open now to allow a refreshing ocean breeze inside. A champagne bucket with ice rested on the glass-topped coffee table where a fine bottle of sauvignon blanc was chilling. He removed the cork and poured two glasses. After handing one to her, he took the other and settled close beside her. His hip brushed hers and he slid his arm along the sofa's low back without touching her. Though he badly wanted to.

"The mother and child? Are they all right?" he asked.

She nodded. "Actually if it had to happen, this was a good time."

"How so?"

"Because of the symposium, we have OB specialists at our beck and call. Dr. McCullough asked Turner to demonstrate the newest laser cauterization technique to stop excessive bleeding."

"Turner? The man I saw you with today?" The effort he exerted to ask the question in a casual tone was great.

She took a sip of her wine, then one of her eyebrows rose. "Don't pretend you don't know who he is."

"Of course I know him. He is the idiot jackal we need to thank for your presence in El Zafir."

She grinned. "The very one who proposed to another woman instead of me."

For which Kamal was eternally grateful. But the way the doctor had looked at Ali—as if she were a particularly intriguing delicacy—disturbed him. And it pricked his temper that Ali had worked side by side with him today.

"He is the man who hurt you. How can you praise him?"

"Not him. His skill as a doctor."

"Do you find him heroic?"

"In medicine? Yes. As a human being? He's the scuzzy stuff on top of food left in the fridge too long."

"Excuse me?"

"To put it in terms you can relate to—he's a jackal's jackal. So, what did you want to discuss with me?"

He blinked, so caught up in the way his stomach knotted at the thought of her with her former lover, he was unable to follow her swift change of topic. "What?"

"You asked me here because you said there were things you wanted to talk to me about."

"Yes. How inconvenient that you are no longer living in the palace."

"So you *do* miss me?"

"Why do you ask?"

"Your aunt mentioned it. We had a goodbye tea the afternoon I moved back to my apartment and she said of all the royal family, you were going to miss me most."

"Did she?"

Ali nodded. "She told me you discussed your quarrel with your father about helping Johara go to the United States. Princess Farrah said she thought you were pleased I was there to talk with afterward. Was she guessing, or is it the truth?"

"A little of both," he said.

He remembered the encounter and the anger his father had roused in him. The man was unable to see reason where his daughter was concerned. And he'd accused Kamal of being weak in regard to his sister. If the king was aware of his eldest son's tendency to be grateful for Ali's presence and support, he would sincerely doubt Kamal's ability to be a strong leader.

"So, what did you want to talk to me about that was so urgent it required my presence in the palace?" She met his gaze. "Why am I here?"

To keep her away from the American doctor. Kamal wanted her to himself. On top of that, he would not permit her to be hurt again by this man.

"I have many things on my mind. What was it I said?"

"That it had something to do with the dedication," she reminded him.

"Ah, yes." And he knew exactly what he wanted to say. "I wish you to accompany me to the affair."

Ali's eyes widened and he was reminded how beautiful they were. Brown with flecks of green when she was happy and content, gold when she was upset. At the moment they were dark and he couldn't decipher what she was feeling. Or himself for that matter. Ever since this afternoon when he'd seen her with another man, he'd been filled with a terrible sense of uncertainty. The feeling was new to him and he did not care for it. He would take pains to rid himself of it.

"Well," he demanded, his inner turmoil making his tone more harsh than he'd intended. "I merely asked you to accompany me. It's a simple question, not brain surgery. I do not understand why a response would take so long."

"That's because you're a man and a royal."

"I am uncertain what gender or social station has to do with the question."

She took another sip of wine as she studied him. "Then I'll explain it. The dedication is a formal affair. That requires appropriate attire. You're the crown prince, which makes attire even more critical."

"You would look lovely in anything." Or nothing, he thought, his body going hot and hard.

"You're a shameless flatterer. But I think it best that I don't go."

If it was merely about clothes, he could take care of that. If it was because she was unsure about making their relationship a closer, physical one—that was a different matter entirely. The strange emotions he'd felt today watching her with another man convinced him he needed to get on with their affair—and he didn't mean the dedication. He must banish her from his mind in order to get on with his destiny.

He set his glass on the table, then took her empty one and set it beside the other. "We have some unfinished business."

"We do? I don't—"

He leaned in close and watched the pulse point at the base of her throat flutter wildly when he tangled his fingers in her hair. Flecks of brown, green and gold danced in her wide eyes.

"I think this is where we left off when my sister picked a most inconvenient time to go into labor and have her baby."

"Oh," she said, a breathless quality to her voice. "That."

"Yes—that." He smiled. "I do not like loose ends."

"Is that what I am?"

"You are a most unforgettable woman," he said, rubbing the silken strands of her hair.

"And you, sir, are a silver-tongued devil."

He grinned. "I like the sound of that."

"Don't think for a minute that I'm susceptible to your flattery."

"It never crossed my mind," he said, cupping her cheek and delicate jaw in his palm. He brushed his thumb across her lips, fascinated by their lush shape and the way they parted slightly. He felt the subtle increase in her breathing.

Suddenly he could wait no longer to taste her again. Lowering his head, he touched his mouth to hers and felt her sigh, followed by a slight trembling. He shifted his weight as he slid his hand to her waist, drawing her more securely against him. Her arms raised and she looped her hands around his neck, at the same time pressing her soft, gently rounded breasts against his chest.

The movement trapped the breath in his throat and made his heart pound. He traced the seam of her lips with his tongue and she opened, inviting him inside. Not a man to ignore an opportunity, he dipped into the moist, honeyed interior. Shivers shook her when he caressed the roof of her mouth, then she met him in a dizzying duel of tongues.

He gloried in her spirit and fearlessness, meeting him head-on. She was a fascinating blend of innocent boldness. He leaned away from her and lowered his hand to her neck, shoulder, then traced a finger over her chest before settling his palm on her firm young breast. She moaned softly at the contact, firing his blood with the erotic sound as she nestled into his touch.

He could barely draw enough air into his lungs. Coherent thought was difficult when he was around this woman. What was it about Ali that created so deep a yearning, so profound a need? Always he'd been able to avoid such feelings for any woman in particular, yet she made him want to forget all but her. He wanted to make long, slow love to her until she thought of no man but him.

He wished to take her to his bed and learn every lush curve of her body. He longed to overwhelm her senses until she couldn't think straight, let alone deny him what he'd been waiting for so long. He wished the two of them to tangle the sheets and hold each other through the night.

He did not want to let her go.

The thought came to him so suddenly and so urgently he wanted—needed—an answer. He kissed her eyelids, her nose, her jaw and the seductive hollow below her ear. Against her throat he earnestly whispered, "Ali, stay with me tonight."

"Kamal," she breathed. "I can't think when you kiss me like this."

He smiled. "I am glad."

She slid her arms from around his neck and drew air into her lungs. Standing, she said, "I have to go."

He stood, too. "But you just arrived. I have planned dinner—"

"That's not all you've got planned." She turned away before he could read her expression and walked to the door.

Standing behind her, he pressed his hand on the door to keep her from opening it wide. Bending slightly, he brushed his lips to her neck and heard her gasp. "Tell me that my touch does not make you want more."

"Kamal—" His name was a pleading whisper on her lips. "I—I don't know if this is right."

"Of course it is."

"For you maybe. But I'm not so sure about me."

"Let me heal the wounds he made."

Her shoulders tensed, telling him she knew exactly who he meant. "It's not just about what Turner did. It's about me."

"Tell me. I wish to know everything about you. Then I will show you that it is right for both of us."

"I'm not so sure you can."

He studied the slender column of her neck, yearning to taste the softness at the same time he put her misgivings to rest. "Let me try. What is stopping you? I wish only to bring pleasure to both of us."

"Without regard for tomorrow?" she asked. "I just can't. Please. Let me go."

"All right. For now. But this is not the end." He let out a long breath as he removed his hand, giving her the freedom to go.

"Good night," she said, then hurried down the hall.

Kamal closed the door. He walked into the living room and picked up her glass, still bearing the imprint of her lips on the rim. She had the most luscious, desirable mouth. He knew women and he would wager almost anything that she wanted him as much as he wanted her. What was holding her back? Was it seeing her former lover again? Was she still harboring feelings for the jackal's jackal?

He had hoped by this time to have his feelings for the American nurse under control. If anything, he was falling more under her spell. He could not give in to the fascination. He must find a way to convince her to be his. Then he could dismiss her from his mind and get on with the future for which he'd been born.

Ali had just ushered Penny Hassan, wife of Prince Rafiq Hassan, into Dr. McCullough's office in the hospital for her prenatal checkup. The princess by marriage was about halfway through her pregnancy and there was no disrobing involved. Therefore, it was permissible to let Penny have a private moment to discuss whatever she wished with her obstetrician. Ali waited at the nurses' station nearby.

She noticed a newspaper resting beside the computer monitor and the headline caught her eye.

What Kind of Woman Does It Take To Wed a Sheik?

She picked up the paper and scanned the article. It was an interview with Princess Farrah regarding the official dedication and opening of the hospital. The princess praised her nephew for the benevolent work he was doing on behalf of the people. He believed health care was a right for every citizen. Halfway through the piece the interviewer switched gears and asked about the man the press had dubbed "Most Eligible Royal Bachelor."

The princess was quoted as saying that her nephew was busy, so she and the king were compiling a list of women for the crown prince to choose from and a decision would be made quite soon about the woman he would wed. Ali was so engrossed in reading, she was unaware anyone had joined her.

"Interesting article," Penny said, nodding at the paper.

"Yeah."

Ali had difficulty catching her breath. She felt as if a great weight rested on her chest. Intellectually she knew and understood that Kamal had to marry. But seeing the information in black and white had made it real—and for reasons she didn't understand—painful.

"You look shell-shocked."

Ali forced herself to fold the newspaper and set it down, then calmly meet the petite blond woman's blue-eyed gaze. Sympathy stared back at her.

"Why would you think that?" Ali asked.

"It's no secret Kamal is smitten with you."

If Ali wasn't shell-shocked before, she was now. How could this be common knowledge? Of course, she didn't believe Kamal was smitten, but he'd definitely singled her out. "That's not exactly true," she denied.

"I beg to differ. It was clear to me the first time I saw the two of you in the palace gardens, the night of the charity auction. Kamal was trying to convince you to accept a job here. He was intrigued by you then.''

That night was never far from Ali's mind. Shortly after she'd met Penny and Rafiq, Kamal had kissed her in the moonlit garden. And she'd told him point-blank that she had a fiancé. She'd thought it was true, but Turner had proposed to someone better. That night Kamal had shocked and aroused her in equal parts. She'd been surprised and intrigued at his audacity, kissing her when he had every reason to believe she was promised to another man. And aroused by the most thorough, seductive, tempting kiss she'd ever received. But she'd never expected to see him again.

''If he was interested at all, it was only because I turned him down. I'd guess he doesn't hear no very often.''

Although he'd heard it loud and clear last night in his suite. She still wasn't sure where she'd found the strength to step out of his embrace. How had she been able to turn her back on kisses that stoked her desire and grew more sweeping and seductive and tempting than the one before? He'd set her on fire and she'd wanted more.

Penny leaned her elbow on the edge of the nurses' station. ''True. I think the word *no* has been stricken from the royal family vocabulary. After all, here you are. Obviously Princess Farrah convinced you to accept her offer.''

''Yes.'' Ali didn't think it was necessary to go into the fact that she'd followed up on the job offer because she couldn't bear to work in the same hospital after Turner proposed to someone else. The humiliation would have been unbearable. ''Between the generous salary and the potential for adventure, it's the opportunity of a lifetime.''

''I remember that same night I met you, Rafiq said his aunt should be in charge of the country's human resources department. He said she had a talent for recruiting skilled personnel. I'm not sure if you're aware that Crystal and I both met her in New York where an exclusive employment agency had given her a slate of candidates for the position as nanny to Fariq's twins. I arrived late for the interview and Crystal had already been hired. But Princess Farrah and I hit it off and she offered me a job as her assistant.''

''No. I hadn't heard.''

Penny smiled at the memories. ''After I arrived, I was assigned to Rafiq. His father had appropriated his assistant and I replaced him. We didn't find out until much later that his father and aunt were juggling personnel to do some matchmaking. Apparently the princess did the same thing when she hired Crystal.''

''How's that?''

''The king had been out of sorts because of a scandal in the palace. The former nanny had fallen in love with Rafiq. I can't really blame her. I fell for him like a moron on a bungee cord.'' She smiled. ''Anyway, the king ordered that a plain woman be hired to fill the position because he thought that would put the lid on palace hanky-panky. That was fine with Fariq because he'd been burned by love and wasn't anxious to do it again. But Crystal badly needed the job and toned down her looks by wearing ugly glasses, going without makeup and wearing frumpy clothes.''

''And Fariq saw through it?''

''Are you kidding? He's a man,'' she said with a grin. ''But Princess Farrah saw through it right away.

Later we learned she'd decided on the spot that Crystal
was the one for Fariq and hired her in order to throw
them together.''

"Very interesting."

"Actually, the interesting thing is that Princess Farrah recruited you as well."

Ali blinked. "I don't get it."

"She's matchmaking again," Penny said.

"That's what the article says. But it's got nothing to
do with me."

"And why would you think that?"

"Because right there in print it says that Princess
Farrah and the king have been in negotiations regarding
the crown prince's bride with the royal families of
neighboring countries."

"So?"

"So, it's clear they intend for him to marry a princess. That proves your theory wrong," Ali pointed out.

"Crystal and I are Americans. We're both so far
removed from royalty it isn't funny. And we married
princes. I stand by my speculation."

"But neither of your husbands is the crown prince
who will inherit the throne. Besides that, he's expected
to provide a future heir for the line of succession. The
woman who has that baby will be a princess."

"That's what I thought. Crystal, too." A faraway
expression crept into her eyes, as if she was remembering. "The night of the charity auction, Crystal
helped me with my hair and makeup. I was too nervous
about attending the event to wonder how someone who
pulled her hair back in such an unattractive bun and
didn't use cosmetics could work magic with *my* ap-
pearance." She sighed as if recalling a wonderful
memory. "Anyway, after she finished with me, she

warned me not to fall in love at the ball like Cinderella. She said, 'Life isn't a fairy tale. When the clock strikes midnight, nothing changes—not even the pumpkin. You come back to your room, take off the party dress and go to work in the morning. Girls like us don't marry handsome princes,'" she finished quoting. "But both of us did."

"And your point would be?" Ali asked.

"You're half in love with Kamal. Like I said before, it's no secret he's been singling you out. You could be the third desert bride. The one who would one day be queen."

Ali shook her head. She had no intention of sharing that Kamal had singled her out, but not with promises of love and forever. He'd tempted her with the offer of an affair.

"Even if what you say is true, Kamal is the crown prince. He might dally with me, but you can bet your glass slippers that he'll marry a princess. The mother of his children will have royal blood."

Penny shook her head and tossed a waist-length strand of blond hair over her shoulder. "I'm not so sure. Crystal and I both have ordinary backgrounds, very common. It's my opinion that Princess Farrah deliberately chose women like us for her nephews, commoners who would bring balance to the princes and not let them get too full of themselves. Obviously you're a working girl, just like we were."

Ali nodded reluctantly. "But I still think you're wrong. When Kamal assumes the throne, there will be a princess of royal blood by his side."

Penny shrugged. "Time will tell." She looked at her watch. "This conversation is so fascinating, but I've got to run and meet Rafiq for lunch. He wants to know how my checkup went.''

"How did it go?''

"Fine as usual.''

Ali nodded. "I'm glad.''

"Will I see you at the dedication ceremony?'' Penny asked.

It was six days away. But who was counting? "No.''

"That's too bad. I was looking forward to seeing you there. Bye, Ali.''

Ali watched the slender woman get into the elevator then the doors whispered shut. There was no point in telling her Kamal wouldn't want her there after the way she'd left him last night. But there had been no choice. She'd finally realized she couldn't have an affair with him. She couldn't give her body unless her heart went along, too. And she wouldn't give her heart unwisely.

She couldn't afford to hope for more with the crown prince because she wasn't the sort of woman who would attract his kind of guy. Turner had taught her that. She needed someone average, regular, someone ordinary like her. And there was no way Kamal would ever be ordinary.

However, he was attracted to her. She had vivid memories of soul-stirring kisses to prove it. But between them, it could never be more than temptation and fascination. He believed that to fulfill the promise of his birth, he wasn't allowed to fall in love. And she didn't want to marry him even if he did. Right?

She wasn't so sure about that anymore. But it was obvious they'd reached a stalemate. This powerful attraction she felt for him hadn't been a waste of time. It had made her realize that when she was ready and the right guy came along, she wouldn't settle for less than being loved for herself. Kamal was the wrong man because he couldn't promise her more than a passionate attachment of limited duration.

He'd drawn a line in the sand when he'd proposed an affair instead of marriage. And she'd decided she couldn't cross it.

Chapter Nine

The following day a rack of designer gowns arrived at Ali's apartment. Kamal had sent them for her to try on. She finally did so, even though she wouldn't be needing one for the dedication ceremony, now five days away.

She looked at herself in the full-length mirrored wardrobe doors hiding the walk-in closet in her bedroom. The gown's full skirt brushed against her white quilt with the patchwork wedding-ring pattern that covered her queen-size four-poster cherry-wood bed. It was impossible to ignore the contrast between pretentious and practical. Not unlike herself and the crown prince.

After she'd left his suite in the palace the night before last, she would have thought he'd gotten the message. But after Penny left the hospital, a woman had cornered Ali in her office and announced she was going to take her measurements. The woman had explained she'd been ordered by Crown Prince Kamal Hassan to

send Miss Ali Matlock a rack of designer dresses and
she needed to know her size. Ali was to choose one
from among them to wear when she accompanied him
to the hospital dedication ceremony. Stunned by the
surprise, Ali hadn't protested being measured. But a
little while ago she'd tried to refuse the delivery and
been categorically ignored.

She knew he was upping the stakes. Would he never
give up? Although, in all fairness, she hadn't actually
turned him down. But this was nothing more than cou-
ture blackmail. Looking at herself in the mirror, she
realized it was very effective. It was difficult to resist
throwing herself at his feet when the strapless, pink
tulle, full-skirted dress with appliquéd flowers trimmed
in silver sequins made her feel like a princess.

That reminded her of the newspaper article and she
realized soon he would have to admit defeat. When he
married there would be no more question about pur-
suing her. Unless maybe, unlike her, the royals could
carry on with that sort of thing.

When he'd first suggested an affair, she'd thought
she might be sophisticated enough to play the game for
the sake of her adventure. But she'd realized she
couldn't separate body and soul. She wasn't willing to
sacrifice her principles for passion that would be fleeting at best.

She looked at herself from every angle, craning her
neck as she tried to see herself from the back. Sighing,
she thought what a shame she would never wear this
fabulous dress in public. Even if she could afford to
buy it on a whim, the odds were good when she returned to real life in Texas, there wouldn't be much of
an opportunity to get gussied up.

She was so immersed in fantasy, the knock on her

door almost didn't penetrate her haze. When it did, her eyes widened. She wasn't expecting anyone. Maybe it was a door-to-door salesman. Was there such a thing in this country? Maybe she should just ignore it.

Lifting her skirt, she hurried down the short hall and turned left past the bar separating the living room from the kitchen. Standing on the wooden floor in the entry, hesitation made her catch her lip between her teeth. Another knock startled her, making her jump. Apparently whoever was there wasn't going away. She would feel incredibly silly opening the door in a designer gown. It was like being caught playing dress-up in her mother's clothes. Another knock nudged her to say something.

"Who's there?"

"Kamal."

She sighed and looked heavenward, feeling like Eve in the Garden of Eden. The apple had been offered and on the other side of her door was the handsome devil who'd dangled it in front of her—in the form of the most beautiful dresses she'd ever laid eyes on. Why hadn't she realized he might show up? And now that he knew she was home, there was no choice. She couldn't leave him standing outside. It was rude. Even if he had caught her in the act of giving in to his temptation by trying on the gowns.

She plastered a big smile on her face, then opened the door. "Hi."

He stood there looking like an ad for *Gentleman's Quarterly*. In his dark suit with white shirt and red tie, he'd definitely dressed the part of the dashing devil she'd thought him moments before. Especially the handsome part.

He studied her with a lazy, appreciative thoroughness that raised a flush on her skin, which he probably noticed considering the way he was staring at the exposed flesh above the gown's bodice. His eyes took on a smoky gleam as he glanced down the full skirt of the dress to her bare feet peeking from beneath the hem. A smile of pure infuriating male satisfaction curved the corners of his mouth.

"May I come in?"

"Of course." She backed up, allowing him to enter, her heart pounding so hard she was surprised he couldn't hear it.

"This is a very pleasant apartment," he said, turning to meet her gaze.

"It's quite comfortable."

She looked around trying to see the place through his eyes. Just beyond the entryway stood a dining table and matching hutch. On the long wall rested a sofa with a glass-topped coffee table in front and two end tables on either side of it. A television was placed on the angled wall across from the bar. It was average, ordinary, which suited her. But the entire place—two bedrooms, one bath, kitchen, living room and dining room—would easily fit into the living room of the suite she'd occupied at the palace. And she especially missed the view of the ocean she'd had. Yet another reminder of the contrasts between them.

"You look completely and utterly charming," he said. He folded his arms over his chest as he studied her.

She wanted to hide her chest, but she wouldn't let him know how he unsettled her. Instead, she put her hands on her hips, trying not to appreciate the feel of the gown's sumptuous material. "Don't think I don't know what you're up to."

He spread his arms wide in the universal I've-got-nothing-to-hide gesture. "But I am not up to anything."

"The last time we were together—"

"Yes?" One dark eyebrow rose as his eyes smoldered with intensity, letting her know he remembered the kiss they'd shared.

She remembered too, every visceral detail in full and vibrant color. If she didn't, this would be so much easier. Because she wanted to kiss him again. She ached to be in his arms, pressed to his chest. She longed for his touch, all over her body. And none of the above was possible.

"I told you I had nothing fancy enough to wear to the dedication ceremony."

"I remember."

"You sent that woman to measure me and the next thing I know there are a dozen ball gowns in my bedroom."

"This disturbs you?"

"Yes."

"Then you are the first woman I have ever met who objects to pretty dresses."

"It's not the dresses I object to but the obvious manipulation tactic that it is."

"Explain please."

"You're trying to coerce me into going to the affair with you." When his eyes glowed at her choice of words, she knew she'd blundered badly. "The ceremony," she said, making things worse.

"I am merely removing any obstacles that prevent you from agreeing to accompany me. You are free to refuse my invitation."

"You knew I wouldn't be able to resist trying on the dresses."

The man truly was a devil. What kind of woman would she be if she said no to this spectacular dress? Females everywhere would think she'd lost her mind. But the dress wasn't the real issue. It was just another way to pump up the volume, increase the pressure, tempt her into taking their relationship up a notch. God help her, it was working. She wanted to go out with him, be with him.

"I suspected you might enjoy the opportunity to wear the gowns. That is all. I would never force you to do anything against your will."

"But I have no place to wear this dress. I didn't agree to attend the event with you."

"Ah, but you didn't say no either. You said only that you had nothing appropriate to wear to the gala."

He had her there. She'd figured her actions would speak louder than words. She'd figured wrong.

"I still have nothing to wear," she said. Holding the sides of her skirt out, she said, "I'm sure this little number and all the others on the rack have a price tag that is beyond my budget."

"What if there is no cost?"

"But surely— There must be—" She stared at him. "It can't be free."

"It can if the designer gives it to you."

"And just why would she do that?"

"If you wear it to a public function and are photographed at my side, you will be responsible for her receiving much free publicity."

"And why would I want to do that?"

"This designer is a local talent my aunt Farrah has taken a fancy to. She's just beginning to make a name for herself in the fashion industry and the right gown on the right woman could secure her future success.''

"So I wouldn't just be turning you down. Like ripples on a pond, my decision would affect Princess Farrah and someone she's taken under her wing.''

"Just so.''

Ali shook her head. Now what? She was reluctant to be with him outside of work. He unsettled her in a primal, sensual way that was dangerous. She'd planned to say no, but he'd made it impossible for her to do it gracefully. And she would be lying if she said she didn't want to go to the gala. But there was one thing he needed to know before she agreed.

"Kamal, do you remember I said I would get back to you on the offer you made me?''

"Every day,'' he said, his eyes like hot coals.

"Well, my answer must be no.''

His lips compressed into a straight line. "I see.''

"No, I don't think you do. I'm just not the type. It's not me, not my style. I'm looking for something permanent and satisfying with a regular guy.''

"Am I not a regular guy?''

She laughed. "You couldn't be average if your life depended on it. So an affair just won't work for me.''

He nodded. "And you think saying this will make me rescind my invitation to the dedication?''

"I just thought you should know in case you wanted to withdraw it.''

"No. I still wish you to accompany me.''

"Then I accept.''

"And I wish you to wear that dress.'' He looked at her chest and if possible, his eyes grew darker.

"But it's not conservative,'' she protested.

"It will be when you wear the matching shawl to

conceal your lovely skin from the gazes of other men who will be present.''

"How did you know there was a matching shawl?''

"I picked this dress out personally before it was sent to you.'' He grinned.

Her heart beat faster as the intense look in his eyes stole the air from her lungs. Every time she was in his presence, she could feel him drawing her in like a baby calf lassoed by a rodeo cowboy. Somehow she had to summon the strength to break away before he roped and hog-tied her heart.

Ali hadn't seen Kamal except at a distance since the night he'd dropped by her apartment five days before. Now here she was ready to exit the limousine and go to the ball, so to speak. It was the hospital dedication ceremony and they hadn't arrived in a pumpkin-turned-coach, but she felt a lot like Cinderella. Especially the part where she brushed shoulders with the crown prince.

She could feel the heat from his body and it warmed her clear to her silver sandal-covered toes. Ever since he'd collected her at her apartment, all her nerve endings had been on full tactical alert. God help her, he looked more handsome in his traditional black tuxedo than she'd ever seen him.

She was nervous about the event, but not nearly as much as she'd expected as she took Kamal's hand to step out of the car. Maybe clothes *did* make the woman. She felt wonderful in this dress, even with the matching shawl discreetly covering her shoulders and bosom. And who knew pink could be a power color? She would never be a princess, but in this dress, she felt like one.

Kamal's fingers pressed her own reassuringly as he tucked her white-gloved hand into the bend of his elbow.

"You look ravishing," he said.

"So do you."

He laughed. "I'll take that as a compliment."

"It was meant as one." He would never know how much.

But the heated, intense expression in his eyes when he looked at her made her heart race.

"It is time to face the world. Are you ready?" he asked. "Do not be nervous."

"Is that a royal order?"

His teeth flashed white. "It is, indeed."

Then they turned and the crush of photographers and reporters gathered to cover the event went into action.

Flashes went off nearly blinding her. Kamal's security staff pressed the crowd back, forming a sort of aisle for them. As they walked past, she heard the whispers. Who is she? Never seen her before. Heard he'll marry soon. Is she the one? The next queen? If they only knew she was Ali Matlock, a nobody from Nowhere, Texas. The thought made her smile, setting off another burst of flashbulbs. If she had a single photogenic gene, she hoped it would do her proud now.

Kamal whisked her into the building adjacent to the hospital that was part administration offices and part educational facility. There was a large room where tables had been arranged in front of a dais. As they moved through the crowd already gathered, she saw the familiar faces of the doctors who had attended the week-long series of lectures. Beside them were the women she assumed were their wives or significant others. Then she spotted Turner—standing with a flute of champagne in his hand.

He was all alone. She'd seen him off and on all week, but had deliberately not brought up the subject of his fiancée. Partly because she didn't want to hear anything about her and partly because she wanted to pretend it truly was past history as she'd said.

But now it was glaringly obvious Turner's fiancée hadn't accompanied him on the trip. What was up with that? When their gazes met, he smiled and lifted his glass in salute. She nodded, then looked up at Kamal and noticed the muscle in his jaw contract as he glared at the other man.

Then he led her to the front of the room. The rest of the royal family was already seated at the head table. When she and Kamal joined them, the invited guests took their places and dinner was served. Ali was too excited to eat and tried to imprint every sensual impression—the crystal sconces on the walls, the floral scent mixed with the fragrance of candles. In the corner on a dais a string trio played flawlessly, giving the event an air of subtle elegance. Circular tables were covered with spotless white tablecloths, set with china trimmed in gold and bracketed with matching forks and knives. It was a world she wouldn't see again and the thought made her a little sad.

Finally, Kamal was introduced and he read some prepared remarks. When he'd finished, he looked at the audience and said, "It is my pleasure to dedicate the Daria Hassan Memorial Hospital in memory of my late stepmother. And I pledge to you that we will channel its resources into the fight against disease and for the preservation of life. Thank you all for coming."

Applause erupted in the room and Ali looked up at

him from where she sat beside the lectern. Emotion swelled in her chest, which could be why she recognized it in his eyes. He'd achieved his goal. And it had been a major commitment of time, energy and resources. But he hadn't let up. Only a man capable of deep feelings could have accomplished such an undertaking. He might try to compartmentalize his emotions, but he couldn't do it indefinitely. She believed he could and would fall in love now that he'd made his dream a reality. But the man who would be king wouldn't give that love to an unsuitable woman. Like her.

Again a sensation of sadness washed over her.

Kamal was surrounded by members of the press seeking quotes from the crown prince and other members of the royal family for their papers and news programs. No one would miss her and she suddenly needed some air. Finding the exit, she made her way to a secluded outside area.

It was a garden lush with plants and fragrant flowers. In the center stood an artfully lighted sculpture and directly across from it was a plaque to Kamal's mother. Around the perimeter, stone benches were placed and discreet white lights illuminated the area like a magic fairyland. The cool air felt wonderful against her heated skin and the serenity of the setting washed over her, seeping into her soul.

"Hello, Ali."

Whirling, she met the man's gaze. "Turner." So much for serenity.

"You look terrific." He walked closer and stopped in front of her.

"Thank you."

It was on the tip of her tongue to say the same to him, but the words wouldn't come. He looked good in his dark suit and charcoal tone-on-tone matching shirt and silk tie. Once upon a time, this man had been ''the one.'' She'd thought she loved him. He was still blond, blue-eyed, Robert Redford-in-his-younger-days hand-some. He was a gifted, skilled, respected doctor, in-tense when he fought to save a life. She waited for her stomach to jump and her hands to sweat. But it didn't happen.

Because he wasn't Kamal.

Now, *there* was a man who embodied the word *in-tensity*. He was handsome as sin, far more exciting and responsible for the lives of every man, woman and child in his country. She couldn't resist comparing the two, but in the end there was really no comparison.

''Tell me, Turner. How is your fiancée? What's her name? Lynnda?''

''Fine.'' He lifted one broad shoulder in a casual shrug. ''The staff back at the hospital won't believe how our little Ali cleans up.''

She tried to smile. ''Have the two of you set a date for the wedding yet?''

He shook his head. ''So tell me what's with you and the prince?''

''We're friends.'' The words felt like a lie, but she didn't know what else to call them. Definitely not lov-ers, and not for lack of his trying.

''I was surprised you went halfway around the world to work. Are you happy here in El Zafir?''

''Very.'' And she found that was definitely true. She loved her job and the people she worked with as well as the patients. Careerwise, she'd never felt more ful-filled. Personally... That was a different story and one she didn't plan to share with him. ''But you—'' She held out one hand. ''You must be excited. Marriage is quite an adventure. And for a man who delivers babies for a living, you must be anxious to start a family.''

"I'm in no hurry." His lips compressed into a straight line. "I'd rather talk about you. What's it like to rub elbows with royalty?''

She remembered rubbing shoulders in the limo and the heat that had followed. Memories of rubbing lips with Kamal flashed into her mind, but she wasn't about to share that either. "Interesting," was all she could think of to say.

"Have you been to the palace?"

She nodded. "I actually stayed there for a couple of weeks.''

"I'm sure the prince found that cozy," he said sarcastically. "Is it called shacking up when it's the palace?''

"I was there in an official capacity," she said coldly.

"As a nurse? Why?"

"I'm not at liberty to say. And I want to hear about you and Lynnda. Doesn't she want children? Is her biological clock ticking?''

"I have no idea." His voice was curt, abrupt, as if he didn't want to talk about it.

Suddenly Ali got it. He'd been dumped by the woman he'd dumped her for. "Lynnda gave you the heave-ho.''

Anger was quick in his eyes. "I was the one who broke it off." There was a defensive note in his voice. "It wasn't right. I knew it after you ran away—"

"I didn't run," she snapped. "I took advantage of a career opportunity.''

"One you originally turned down," he reminded her. "Because we were together.''

"Things have a way of working out for the best.''

He shook his head. "Not this time. I realized after you were gone that I missed you." He reached out and curved his long fingers around her upper arms. "I should have asked you to marry me, Ali."

"Don't, Turner—"

"I was stupid. I should have proposed to you when I could have. Do you think I came here for the symposium? It's because of you, Ali." There was a desperate look in his eyes as he leaned forward. "Give me another chance. Tell me it's not too late for us."

Ali would have dodged the kiss except that he held her still. When his lips touched hers, she waited for the old feelings he'd once generated to come again. But she felt nothing. Except pity and sadness for him.

"No, Turner—" She pulled away and forced him to break his grip on her arms. "It's way past too late."

"You don't mean that." Astonishment made his eyes wide.

"I've never been more sure of anything in my life."

"But why? Is there someone else?"

"No. I've just moved on," she said.

"It's because of the prince," he accused. "There's something going on between the two of you, isn't there?"

"No."

She wanted to tell him it was because he was a social-climbing manipulator and she counted her blessings that she'd escaped him. But that served no purpose. He'd hurt her, but she felt no inclination to hurt back. She felt nothing at all. And that's how she knew not only that she was over him, but that she'd never loved him at all.

"You're lying, Ali. Little Miss Nobody is clutching

the prince's coattails. A man like that will chew you up and spit you out. He's not your type.''

The fact that he was right in no way softened her reaction to him. How could she have *ever* thought she cared about this man? Fortunately time and distance had shown her the truth. She'd never have been happy with someone who would always make her question how he was using her. He wasn't worth any further effort.

''I have to go back inside,'' she said coldly.

Turner blocked her path when she tried to go past him. ''I have more to say.''

''Ali?'' The edgy hostility in Kamal's voice carried from the other side of the garden. He moved quickly across the space separating them and stopped beside her.

''Kamal— I mean, Your Highness,'' she said, remembering the proper form of address when they were not alone.

Kamal wanted to take the other man apart with his bare hands. He'd heard part of the doctor's venomous words to her and suspected he'd kissed Ali. The blood boiled through his veins and made him sorry this wasn't a hundred years ago and he wasn't civilized. But he'd worked too long and hard, to spoil the hospital's triumphant evening with a brawl.

He lifted her hand and bent to touch his lips to her knuckles. Straightening, he said, ''You have been away from me for too long. I cannot bear your absence a moment longer. You'll excuse us, Doctor?'' He infused the word with contempt.

Without waiting for the other man to reply, he tucked Ali's hand in the bend of his elbow and led her from the garden. But he wasn't quite ready to take her back inside. There was a patio just outside the room where the gala was still under way. Music drifted to them.

He stopped and looked down at her. "May I have this dance?"

"Of course. You're my hero. My knight in shining armor. My champion."

Self-satisfaction raced through him. But as calmly as possible he said, "How so?"

She placed her small hand in his and her palm on his shoulder as he pulled her to him and started to move in time with the waltz music.

"He wanted me back," she said simply.

Anger and rebellion roared through him at the very idea. The thought of her in another man's arms was unthinkable. White-hot fury lasered through him. He could not bear to think of her with anyone else.

"And you do not wish to go?" he asked, again as serenely as he could.

"No. He blew it."

Her words made the corners of his mouth turn up. "Indeed he did," he said, pulling her more possessively to him.

The question was, how was he, Kamal, going to avoid "blowing it" with her? She had refused his offer of an affair. Instead of cooling his ardor, he wanted her. If anything, he wanted her more ardently.

Which meant after this night she would be an even greater distraction. As he gazed into her lovely face, he realized it was imperative to find some way to come to terms with this increasing sense of uncertainty where she was concerned.

No other woman had made him feel these things, and he would find a way to put a stop to it with Ali.

Chapter Ten

Curled up on her bed in her robe, Ali heard the knock on her apartment door and decided not to answer it. She didn't particularly care who was there. The shock of the news story she'd seen on CNN earlier in the day hadn't gone away. Reporters had shown footage of the hospital dedication from the night before and focused on Kamal—his marriage prospects.

The information had surprised her, then sort of de-sensitized her emotions, yet there was pain beyond this numbness scratching to get in and she was trying to keep it away as long as possible. Fortunately, getting through the rest of her workday had forced her to focus her attention elsewhere. But as soon as her shift had ended, she'd left the hospital and the feelings closed in on her.

The comfort of her robe and slippers as she curled in the fetal position was just what the doctor or-dered. If only there was some prescription medication she could take to start her heart healing. Stupid,

stupid thought. Somehow she knew she would never be over this.

Another knock sounded, more insistent than the first. Someone wanted her to answer. The last time this had happened, Kamal had been there. The memory brought a fresh wave of pain to her heart and tears to her eyes. It couldn't be him. According to rampant gossip, he would have no reason to darken *her* door again.

She sat up in bed and swung her legs over the side. Waiting through several moments of silence, she hoped whoever was there had taken the hint and taken a hike. But another rapping commenced and whoever was doing it wasn't happy.

"That makes two of us," she mumbled.

She padded out of her bedroom, down the hall and through the living room to the small entryway. As much as she didn't want to open up, she was concerned the noise would bother her neighbors, many of whom worked until all hours at the hospital. If anyone was trying to sleep, she didn't want them disturbed just because she wasn't feeling social enough to answer her door.

In case she didn't want to talk to the someone there, it crossed her mind to look through the peephole. But it seemed whoever had installed the sucker was a giant and she didn't feel like dragging over a step stool. After removing the chain from the lock, she turned the knob and opened the door a crack, then her heart cracked a little more.

"Are you ill?" Kamal asked, his gaze raking her from the top of her head over her white chenille robe to the tips of her fuzzy yellow slippers.

"No." Unless you counted a battered spirit. On the upside, because her spirit had taken a hit, she couldn't find the will to care that he was seeing her at her tackiest.

She wanted to be rude and shut the door in his face, but that was unfair. It was okay for her to be upset, but not with him. He'd never lied. He'd been straightforward and honest with her from the very beginning. She took in the sight of him and wished she could hate him. But just her bad luck, the opposite was true and she was stunned by the bone-deep pain slicing through her.

All along she'd thought she was too smart to fall for him. She'd let him talk her into anything by letting herself believe it was just part of the adventure. Now she knew that in spite of all her warnings, she'd harbored the hope of something more with Kamal. For all her hot air about love being an involuntary reaction, she'd tried to control her feelings. Just like him. Unlike him, she'd failed miserably.

From the starched collar of his white dress shirt, down to his conservative navy tie and expensive pin-striped suit, he was every inch the man who would be king. And she cared a lot for the man who cared so deeply about his people that he couldn't love her.

"What is the matter with you?" he asked, studying her. There was concern in his dark eyes and it made her want to cry again.

"What makes you think something's wrong?"

"You are dressed for bed and it is early yet."

She lifted one chenille-clad shoulder. "It was a hard day. I just wanted to come home and veg out."

That was the honest truth. Days tended to be hard when your heart was breaking. It took a lot of energy to hide that from co-workers and patients. She just wanted to sleep, if she could, and find blessed relief.

"You should have informed me that you were going to miss the employee appreciation dinner at the hospital."

"Why would you need to know?"

His chin lifted slightly. "I am the crown prince."

That lame excuse fell into the "just because" category and she didn't have the energy to debate him. "It slipped my mind," she lied.

The truth was, she'd known he would be there to say a few words to all the employees and she couldn't face him. Because the tears that were filling her eyes now, at the sight of him, would have happened then in a very public and humiliating way. She cursed herself for being unable to stop them.

"Enough." Kamal settled his palm against the door and pushed it wide, then shut it behind him. "What is wrong?"

"Nothing."

"Do not tell me this." He gripped her arms, not in a hurtful way, but firm. To break his hold would require more effort than she could muster. "You are crying and I wish to know why."

She shrugged and managed a small smile. "It's just a female thing. I'm feeling a little blue. I get this way sometimes and it's best to just give me my space. Sorry about the meeting. Thanks for stopping by, but I'll be fine—"

"Stop." He gave her a gentle shake. "You are not the kind of woman who weeps and wails and ignores her duty. I insist you tell me what is going on. I see the tears in your eyes. Did something happen at the hospital? To one of your patients? Is it the jackal? Has he contacted you? I wish to hear why you are upset. Out with it."

She so didn't want to talk to him *about* him. It would only make things worse. Why couldn't he just go away and let her grieve in private?

"Look, Kamal, it's not about work. It's personal—"

"It *is* him. What did he do to hurt you?"

Her eyes widened. The symposium had ended two weeks ago. She hadn't seen or heard from Turner since the night of the dedication. They were so over. No way could anything Turner Stevens did make her cry.

"No." She shook her head. "He can't hurt me ever again, thanks to you."

How ironic. That night in the hospital's memorial garden, Kamal had been her hero. Yet thoughts of his dashing deeds made her eyes fill again. A single fat tear slid down her cheek and plopped on the breast of her soft, fuzzy robe.

He ran his fingers through his hair. "Then tell me, Ali. You are making me crazy. Someone hurt you."

"You're jumping to conclusions. You don't know that."

"You are wrong. You were lying when you said the meeting slipped your mind. You're not a good liar, which I like very much. But that means you are running from something that is causing you pain."

"Running?" She blinked at his odd choice of words. "What are you talking about?"

One dark eyebrow rose as if to say this is me. "You pursued a job in my country after turning it down because you were running from the pain of a man's betrayal." He lifted one broad shoulder in a casual shrug. "After their divorce, your mother ran away from your father, severing her own ties, and yours as well. Now you have run from a hospital function."

She put her hands on her hips. "Who sprinkled you with psychobabble dust?"

"It does not take a degree in psychology to see the pattern. This behavior of running away when you are hurt is what you learned as a child."

Now that he pointed it out, she knew he was right. And she responded like the mature, health-care professional that she was. "So?"

"So now I will know this man's identity. I will make him sorry he hurt you. I will make him sorry he was ever born." His eyes darkened as he met her gaze. "I demand to know his identity. His name, Ali. Now."

She stared at him, unable to look away. One of the things she both loved and hated about him was his iron will. He wasn't going to let this drop, so she might as well get it over with. "His name is Kamal Hassan."

"Me?" He took half a step back as if she'd struck him. "I do not understand."

"I have to sit." Suddenly she felt as if her legs wouldn't hold her. Turning away, she walked to the beige sofa and sat down.

He followed and sat beside her, half turned toward her. "Explain."

"On CNN today I saw— They said you're going to announce your engagement to Princess Mikayla Sharif from some neighboring country that I can't remember the name of." She met his gaze, grateful that her own wasn't blurry with tears. "So I guess congratulations are in order."

"You think I am engaged?"

"It's not a stretch, Kamal. I've known all along you were going to marry."

"Then why are you suffering?"

Just like a man. Worse than most. Not only wasn't

he making this easy, he wanted to talk about it. Since when did a man want to discuss touchy-feely stuff? Best say it straight out, get it over with so he could leave her in peace.

"I'm hurt because you're going to marry someone else and I've fallen in love with you. There, now you can go."

He looked only slightly less stunned than when she'd said he was the man who'd hurt her. He nodded slowly and thoughtfully.

"I have a solution to your discomfort," he said after several moments.

"There is no solution. And don't tell me time will make me feel better. It's probably the truth, but you don't owe me anything. You've never lied to me or led me to believe you could give anything beyond an affair. So, let's just say it's been fun and go our separate ways."

"I have a better idea."

"Of course you do." She sighed. "And what would that be?"

"You will marry me."

"What?" Now it was her turn to be stunned. She couldn't believe her ears were working right. And if she hadn't already been sitting down, she probably would have collapsed at his feet.

"I wish you to marry me. It is the perfect answer."

"But you're engaged to someone else." The story of her life. "The king— Your aunt— Obviously they chose someone for you. I heard—"

He shook his head. "I know nothing of this and if someone had been selected by my father, I would have been the first to know. The information would not come from the news media. I am making my choice now. Again I say, I wish for you to marry me."

She studied the earnest expression on his face. "If I didn't know better, I'd say you were serious."

"I am quite serious. This is not a matter for humor."

No. He'd made that clear. So he must be sincere. The veil of darkness surrounding her instantly lifted and disappeared. Suddenly the weight of the world fell from her shoulders and happiness seemed to explode inside her.

He reached out and took her hands in his, then lifted her left and placed a kiss on the ring finger. Her heart raced a hundred miles an hour.

His eyes smoldered as he looked at her. "Marry me, Ali," he said, his voice husky and grave.

The three words she'd longed for and never expected to hear. What else could she say? "Yes," she whispered.

He grinned as he nodded with satisfaction. "We will be married as soon as the arrangements can be made." He stood and pulled her to her feet and into his arms. "You will make an exemplary queen."

Then he lowered his head and pressed his mouth to hers. She was awash in sensation, bombarded with feelings and in a state of sensory overload. And happier than she'd ever believed possible.

Kamal sat behind his desk with the same smile he'd been wearing all morning. Last night Ali accepted his proposal. He'd dispensed with the terrible feeling of uncertainty he'd experienced after seeing her with another man.

Ali was his. The thought made his grin wider.

Emir appeared in the doorway to his office. "Your Highness, Miss Matlock is here to see you."

Pleasure filled him at the prospect of seeing her sooner than this evening. His customary response was to question the feeling—deny it or push it away—but he couldn't manage it. His inability to control the feeling disturbed him.

"Send her in, Emir."

Moments later, Ali entered the room and his assistant closed the door. As always, his breath caught at the sight of her, lovely in a green ankle-length, long-sleeved knit dress belted at her slender waist. He was drawn to her like a man lost in the desert is attracted to an oasis. Again, the power of the sensation made him uneasy.

He stood up and rounded his desk. "Why are you here? Although it pleases me to see you," he added.

"I need to talk to you," she said, smiling uncertainly.

Kamal studied her large, expressive eyes because he knew the mercurial shading was a barometer of her mood. Today there was little gold shimmering in their depths. They were a beautiful, dark shade of brown and made him tense.

"What is it, Ali?"

"I—" She stopped and swallowed. "It's—" She twisted her hands together.

He took her hands in his, then led her to one of the leather wing chairs facing his desk. "Please sit. Whatever it is, you can tell me. We are going to be married."

"About that—" She met his gaze and her eyes were darker than he'd ever seen them. "When you asked me to marry you, I was so happy. The feeling swept me away."

"Good."

She stiffened. "But I've had time to think about it. You never once said how you feel about me."

He had thought they'd said everything necessary, that the situation was under his complete control. Her reaction took him completely by surprise. "Why do you question that? I asked you to marry me and you accepted. There is nothing more to say."

"There's a *lot* more to say."

"Such as?" He leaned a hip against his desk and folded his arms over his chest.

"Why did you propose to me?"

"Why do you ask?"

"Please stop answering my question with a question." She huffed out a breath. "It might work in negotiations with other countries, but it doesn't with me. Why did you ask me to marry you?"

"Because you are everything I require in a wife."

Her eyes grew darker, if possible. "Could you be more specific?"

"You care about my people. Your enthusiasm for your work in the hospital is proof of that. It is also an indication to me that you care about the future of this country. You are quite lovely and very photogenic."

"I clean up pretty well," she agreed, a note of sarcasm in her voice.

He was unsure how to respond and decided straightforward flattery was best. "Just so. After the dedication, reporters were eager to learn the identity of the beauty who accompanied me." He considered her reaction to this compliment. In his experience it was the swiftest way to thaw a woman's pique. He hadn't a clue about why she was vexed, but it was always best to use a proven method. Still, Ali's expression had not softened. This puzzled him greatly.

"Is there anything else?" she asked.

"Yes," he said since she was obviously waiting for more. "You are intelligent."

It would be easier if she were not. Boredom would have beset him very soon after meeting her. But her humor and sharp wit had kept him intrigued.

She smoothed the knit material of her dress across her knees. "Are you finished?"

He could be. Or not, he decided, staring at her stony expression. "You will make a good wife."

"Even though I don't have royal blood? I'm a simple Texas girl."

If her eyes hadn't darkened more and her lush lips had not compressed to a straight line, he might have voiced an objection to that last statement—except the part about Texas. But there was nothing simple about Ali Matlock.

"In spite of what you might think, royal blood is not a prerequisite for a wife. It does not ensure strong, healthy offspring."

"And you think I can—produce hale and hearty children?"

"Yes," he said, more forcefully than he'd meant to. "There is nothing else to say. There are considerations far more important than bloodlines."

"Such as?"

She was relentless. What did she wish him to say that would restore her good humor? Ah. Humor. He'd forgotten. "You make me laugh."

"Do I?" One corner of her mouth tilted up.

She was relenting. He would push the advantage.

Leaning forward, he braced his hands on the arms of her chair, trapping her. "Yes," he said softly as he let his gaze drift over her face.

He kissed the corner of her mouth, then the delicate curve of her jaw and the soft, seductive indentation beneath her ear. The small shudder that shivered through her made him smile.

He stared into her eyes. "I cannot wait to make you mine. You are the perfect woman to be my wife."

He started to kiss her again, but she placed a finger over his mouth. "Don't. I can't think straight when you kiss me."

"You think too much. It is much better to just *feel*."

He lifted her wrist and brought her hand to his lips, kissing the tip of each finger. A purely male satisfaction filled him at her sharply indrawn breath. Then he turned her hand and pressed his mouth to her wrist, savoring the wildly beating pulse there. She might act the cool interrogator, but he knew the hot blood that raced through her veins. And he knew exactly how to make her respond and lose control.

He traced a finger up her arm and she stood abruptly, forcing him to move away from her. "What is it, Ali?"

"Do you love me?" she blurted out.

The knot of uncertainty returned with a vengeance, making him angry. "That is irrelevant," he snapped.

"It's the most relevant issue to me." She took a deep breath. "Last night when you asked me to marry you, I was—overjoyed."

"Good. Now then—"

"I'm not finished. And this is too important to let you steamroll me."

He folded his arms over his chest and leaned a hip against his desk. "All right. Continue."

"I was swept away—miserable one second because I was under the impression you were engaged to someone else and our—what we have—would be over. Then you asked me to marry you and I was on top of the world."

"What is your point?"

"You never said you love me."

"I have told you how I feel about you."

"You listed my positive characteristics like bullets on a résumé. I want to know how you *feel.*"

"I feel exceptional—at least I did before you started this ridiculous conversation."

"You object to personal stuff?"

"Yes." Her question indicated she understood. But the serious expression on her face did not reassure him. "You are the woman I choose to spend my life with."

"The one to whom you would be faithful?" she asked, one dark eyebrow rising questioningly.

"How can you distrust that? I am an honorable man who sets an example for his people. When we take our vows, I will be faithful to you always."

"Because you love me?"

"Because you will be my wife and the mother of my children."

"Fulfilling a duty?"

"Just so," he said, pleased she understood. But when he watched her eyes dim to unfathomable pools of darkness, he knew he'd blundered badly.

Her chin rose a fraction. "Then I must change my mind and decline your proposal."

"Why?" Again he was surprised by her.

"I won't compromise my dreams by settling for less than what I want or deserve."

"You're talking about a declaration of love," he

said angrily. "Last night you did not question it yet you have known all these many weeks my position on this issue."

"Love isn't a political point of view. Without it, marriage would be a charade of duty. Last night I was overwhelmed. Today I can see things more clearly."

"Your behavior makes that statement debatable."

"There are some who would agree with you. But it's clear to me that your vision of marriage makes it a charade of duty. And that's the only way you will ever need me. It's not enough for me. I want more."

"Being my queen isn't adequate? I can give you everything—wealth, material possessions, passion—"

"Without love, it would be just going through the motions. I would take a plumber who loves me unconditionally over a prince who doesn't care about me as more than an obligation." She started toward the door. "Goodbye, Kamal."

"Are you going to ignore the terms of your contract and return home before it is time?"

"You mean, am I going to run away?"

"Yes."

She sighed. "No. For what it's worth, I'll always be grateful to you for making me see the pattern. It's time to break it. No matter how hard it will be to see you—feeling the way I do—I'm going to stay and fulfill my contract."

The haze of his anger did not conceal from him the pain in her face and the strength it took for her to say the words. She was magnificent. Her character and force of will were more qualities that he wanted in his children. But she exhibited stubbornness as well. Not a bad quality if properly channeled. In this instance, he wished it were aimed elsewhere. He could not say what she wished to hear. He could not give in to the weakness and love her.

He nodded. "I am glad you will stay."

She took a step back as if he'd struck her. Any hope lingering in her face died. "I wish I could say the same."

He steeled himself against feeling anything. "I regret any discomfort to you," he said in his most formal voice.

"Discomfort?" She laughed, but there was none of her customary humor in the sound. "That doesn't begin to describe what I feel. It's worse than when my father abandoned me for a new family. It's deeper than what I experienced when Turner stomped on my heart and asked someone more appropriate to be his wife. Worst of all, there's not a single medication to help manage the pain."

"It is your decision."

She took a deep breath. "No. It's yours. But I have to live with it. And so do you."

Then she turned her back on him and left the room.

Kamal stared at the empty space where the flesh and blood, curves and contours, passionate woman had stood moments before and wished for the terrible uncertainty back. He did not like it, but that would be easier to bear than the black void now looming before him.

Chapter Eleven

Kamal glanced at the clock on his desk and sighed. It was after ten and he'd missed dinner again. He rubbed his eyes and set down the financial reports he'd been scanning. Leaning back in his chair, he winced as his muscles protested the movement. He had been hunched over his work too long. But the physical discomfort was nothing compared to the aching loneliness that closed in, as it frequently did, whenever he was unoccupied.

Thoughts of Ali assaulted him. He couldn't work twenty-four hours a day to keep from thinking of her. Living without her was driving him to distraction. Somehow he had to find a way to smooth things over between them and begin again.

"You are still working?"

In the dim light beyond his desk lamp he saw his aunt with his father beside her. "It is late, Aunt Farrah. What are you doing here?"

"It *is* late, my son," his father answered. "That is why we have come. To check up on you."

"There is no reason."

The two of them walked farther into the room. His father stared at him. "Your aunt and I are concerned about you."

Kamal rolled his shoulders, feeling the muscles in his neck and back, still cramped from the position he'd maintained for more hours than he cared to think about. "I do not understand. Everything is fine. There's no cause for concern."

"On the contrary," the king said. "We have heard from your staff—"

"Who?" Kamal asked more sharply than he would have liked. The slip betrayed emotion he was working hard to conceal.

"All of them," his father answered. "For the last two weeks you have been working inhuman hours and expecting your assistants to do the same."

"I would not require of anyone else that which I do not perform myself. And more," Kamal protested.

"That is exactly our point," his aunt chimed in. "You are going to kill yourself with these insane hours. But it cannot be permitted that you take your staff down with you. They are all threatening to quit."

"I'm fine. And I will deal with my employees. Now, if that is all—" He leaned forward, closer to the desk, and started to pick up the report again. But the two hadn't moved. He met their gazes. "What is it?"

His aunt sat in one of the leather wing chairs before his desk. It was the same one Ali had used two weeks before when she'd been here. Ever since, he'd experienced a very large, very black, very bleak emptiness in his days.

The nights were worse—especially the restlessness when missing her threatened to drown him. When he did manage to sleep, dreams of her tormented him.

He had seen her several times from a distance when hospital business had taken him there. But he'd grown accustomed to much closer contact. He felt the lack of their spirited discussions and missed listening to the wisdom of her opinion. His senses were deprived of touching her, inhaling the sweet fragrance of her skin, savoring the warmth of her body. He'd become used to seeing her every day and had looked forward to deep, passionate kisses becoming a part of their time together. None of this could be done from a distance. But to breach it, she wanted his soul. How could he give her that?

"We are not through with you yet," his aunt said. "You are ill-tempered, surly and sarcastic. You lose your composure at the slightest provocation. You are not yourself at all."

"I am the same as I have always been," he said, knowing it was not the truth. But he refused to acknowledge to them that there was any merit in their concerns. Because he would have to be an idiot not to know where they were going with this discussion. And he did not wish to speak of it. Or her. He would handle the situation on his own. Although he had not yet decided on a course of action to convince her to abandon her demand.

Farrah looked at her brother, who sat in the other chair. "He is in denial, Gamil. I think an emotional intervention is the only solution."

"I agree," the king said.

"What are you talking about?" Kamal demanded.

Farrah met his gaze. "Up until two weeks ago you were spending time with Ali Matlock—"

"How do you know this?"

"Please, Kamal." She gave him a wry look. "It's fairly impossible for you to do anything without the rest of the palace knowing about it."

"And what is your point?"

"Two weeks ago," she continued, "I leaked a story to the press of your engagement."

"Why?" He remembered Ali's tears when she'd spoken of it. Then her joy when he'd said she must marry him. And later she'd told him that discomfort didn't begin to describe how she felt after what he'd done to her. The thought of her unhappiness pained him deeply. "Why did you involve the media?" he asked again.

"I was becoming impatient with the amount of time it was taking for you and Ali to state your feelings for each other and get on with it."

"What feelings? Get on with what?" Kamal asked.

"Your aunt is quite the matchmaker," the king interjected. "She is responsible for bringing Penny and Crystal here for your brothers."

She turned her gaze from her brother and looked at Kamal. "Do you recall that after my trip to New York when I hired Crystal and Penny, I stopped in Austin, Texas, to visit with our good friends the Prescotts?"

"I remember."

But Kamal had no idea what this had to do with anything. He wondered if she suspected Johara and her baby were now there and under the protection of the very same family. Sam Prescott, the son of his father's friend, owed him a favor and was sworn not to reveal his sister's whereabouts to anyone without her permis-

sion. But studying his aunt's expression, he decided she
was too preoccupied with other matters. Like matchmaking. He wondered how his revered aunt would deal
with failure where he was concerned if she forced him
to reveal that he intended to handle this situation on
his own.

"During the visit," she continued, "I experienced
chest pain that turned out to be nothing serious. But,
at the Prescotts insistence, I went to the emergency
room. Ali was seeing to a woman in labor. That was
how our paths crossed."

"I don't understand what this has to do with anything, Aunt Farrah."

"It has everything to do with everything. As soon
as I met and got to know her, I was convinced she
would be perfect for you."

"So you offered her a position in the hospital to
bring her here for me," he guessed.

"Yes. And I was right. You fell in love with her."

Kamal shook his head. "I have taken great pains that
such a thing would not happen."

"You are a fool to believe you can control your
feelings this way," his aunt protested.

"So I've been told."

"It is because of me, is it not, my son?" His father
looked at him with great sadness in his dark eyes.
"You believe that because of my behavior after losing
your mother and stepmother, the man who would become the leader of his people cannot put himself at risk
of such weakness?"

"It is an emotional defect not permitted the heir to
the throne of this country."

His father shook his head. "There is no shame in

loving a woman. If she is the right woman, your love will make you stronger.''

"And if you lose that woman?'' Kamal snapped.

His father leaned forward. "That is fate and cannot be controlled. I can only tell you a man is better, more powerful for having the love of a revered woman. I am sure you have heard of the English king who was forbidden to wed the woman he loved because of the traditions of his time. He refused the crown. The next in the line of succession was enthroned.''

"Is there a point to this, Father?''

The king nodded. "Two, actually. First of all, it is not necessary for you to carry the burden of responsibility alone. If you need help, it will be there for you as you were there for me.''

"And the second thing?'' Kamal asked.

"We have no power over chance and circumstance. But to turn your back on a woman you love and who loves you in return is foolishness—a characteristic not valued in a leader.''

"But father—''

He held up his hand and his expression was fierce. "No one knows this better than I—'It is better to have loved and lost than never to have loved at all.'''

Kamal felt a knot of anger in his chest. "Even though that love made you turn your back on a beloved daughter?''

The king rested his elbows on his knees and clasped his hands. He bowed his head. "It was a dark time for me. I did not wish to go on.''

"And she looked so much like her mother the sight of her was a painful reminder of what you'd lost?''

"Yes.'' He shook his head as he looked up. "I am

not proud of this. I blame myself for her rebellion and the results of it.''

"The results are her baby, your grandson," Kamal said.

"Yes."

"You deliberately shut her out, Father, because after suffering the loss of her mother, you were afraid of caring too much. And in doing so, you must take some responsibility for what happened to her."

"I see that now," the older man answered, bowing his head.

"But you never told her this." Kamal felt his anger slipping away. His father's forlorn expression told of the high price he was paying for his stubbornness.

"Have you been in touch with your sister?" Their gazes locked.

"I have."

"She and the baby are well?"

Kamal nodded. "Johara is preparing to go to a university. She plans to earn a degree in business."

The king nodded. "She always talked of continuing her education in the United States. I assume that is where she is?"

"I have promised her that I will not reveal her whereabouts to anyone."

"Even her father?"

"She is concerned that you will coerce her into coming back. Without proof that you have softened your attitude, she refuses to subject her child to an environment such as she left behind."

"I miss her," he whispered.

Kamal studied his father. The love the king felt for his lost daughter was clear in his eyes. In that moment, Kamal realized the man had tried to control his feelings, deny them, turn his back on further weakness. That had been a greater disaster. Johara had suffered and he'd lost the love of this beloved daughter that had once been his for the taking.

"Your father is not perfect," Aunt Farrah said. "He makes mistakes, as he did with your sister. But the test of a strong man, a strong leader, is realizing his errors and making amends."

"Your aunt is right," the king said, smiling wanly at her.

Farrah's chin lifted slightly. "Of course I am. It is time for you to make amends and straighten out your life, Kamal."

"There's nothing wrong with my life," he protested, studying the two of them. Schemers both, he thought, but couldn't find it in him to condemn their actions that had involved the media. "So you leaked a story of my engagement to the press? To move things along? With Ali and myself?"

"Yes," she agreed. "And I demand to know what harm you did to Ali? What have you done to push her away?"

"Me?" he said, annoyed. "What makes you think *I* did anything?"

"Because you are a man. *And* the crown prince. Of course you did something."

"It was what I cannot do that caused a problem," he admitted.

"Tell me," she insisted.

"I refuse to love her," he said.

"I think it is too late for that, my son." The king sighed. "Love is nothing to be ashamed of. Memories of it sustained me through the dark times. I see now that my weakness was not in loving, but refusing to ask for the help I needed.''

"I agree, my brother,'' his aunt said, meeting his father's gaze. Then she turned to him. "Kamal, you fell in love with Ali the first time you saw her.''

Kamal was very much afraid she was correct.

The king rested his forearms on the chair and leaned forward. "Your mother told me once 'to the world you are one person, to one person you are the world.' Twice in my life I felt my world fall apart. The second time you were old enough to step in for me. But that is no excuse for my lapse in judgment about seeking help. You have the support of your brothers always. Do not make the same mistakes I did or you will suffer unimaginable losses such as I have. Do not turn away from the one person who, I feel certain, is your world. A good ruler does not run from a problem, he faces it.''

"Burying yourself in work is the same as running away,'' his aunt interjected. "And I would like to point out that your refusal to say the word *love* will not make the feeling go away.''

Kamal leaned back in his chair. They were right and he knew it. He had tried everything he could to banish the emptiness Ali had left in his world. He'd buried himself in work until he was so exhausted he fell into bed. But rest would not come. He dreamed of her and the wound inside festered and grew more raw.

"I'm not saying you are correct, but for the sake of argument, what do you suggest I do?'' He looked from his father to his aunt.

"You must go to Ali and admit you were wrong,'' Farrah suggested.

"Impossible,'' his father said.

"No," Kamal agreed. "I am never wrong."

"Wisdom dictates we save the debate for another time." She glanced between the two of them and sighed. "I might have known the two of you would stick together."

"Have you another suggestion, Aunt?"

"You must court her." She smiled. "The more I think about it, the more I think this tack would be better than saying you were wrong."

"Court her?" Kamal rested his elbows on his desk.

"Yes. Take her to Paris—the city of love." She tapped her lip. "Better yet, Rome—the city of eternal love. Be romantic. Sweep her away with a proposal of marriage." She sighed.

Kamal decided not to share the fact that he'd swept her away once and still not achieved his desired result. He wished to marry her and spend the rest of his life with her by his side. He would protect her and care for her and give her children. He would be faithful to her always. Why was one small word more important than everything he would do for her?

"Is this how an ordinary man would succeed in marrying her?" he asked them.

The other two glanced at each other with blank expressions. His father shook his head. "I do not believe an ordinary man could—what is the expression—pull it off."

"I agree," his aunt concurred. There was silence for several moments. Finally she said, "I have heard that courting is accomplished with things like flowers and candy."

His father sat up straight. "I believe jewelry is of benefit also. Women like jewelry, do they not, Farrah?"

She smiled and nodded. "Yes, indeed. An excellent suggestion, Gamil. A necklace, bracelet— Or better yet, a ring would definitely work in your favor."

"I have rings," his father said. "I have been saving the one I gave to Johara's mother for her." He looked at Kamal. "But I also have the one that I gave to your mother when she agreed to marry me. It is a most impressive emerald," he said proudly.

"Do not ordinary men give their intended diamonds?" Kamal asked.

Again the two across the desk from him looked at each other with blank gazes. Then the king said to him, "I do not have a frame of reference for ordinary. Why is this so important to you?"

"Because Ali says she wants to marry a regular guy. If I am going to convince her to marry me, that is what I must be."

His aunt nodded. "I understand. Then flowers, candy and a small, tasteful diamond would be best."

Kamal felt the disconcerting uncertainty again. He did not care for it any more now than he had before. But, with luck, he could prove to Ali that he was like every other man. When he'd accomplished that, he could persuade her to say yes once again.

He would not contemplate failure to achieve this objective.

Chapter Twelve

"You look like someone snipped the ears off your favorite stethoscope."

In line to pay for her salad at the hospital cafeteria, Ali glanced behind her. Crystal Hassan stood there with a cup of tea. Ali was off duty after a long day and had hoped to grab something to take home for dinner, and slip out without having to talk to anyone. She needed to garner her strength for tomorrow night when she had to see Kamal at the weekly Quality Council meeting.

Determined not to run away, she had already gone once and it had been harder than she'd imagined. Being in the same room with him, the effort to hide her feelings had been difficult and exhausting. She was going to need all her intestinal fortitude. Because, if nothing else, she was grateful to Kamal for showing her that retreat was cowardly and one had to face one's problems head-on.

She smiled at the other woman. "Hi, Crystal. Are you here for a checkup?"

She shook her head. "I'm visiting my assistant. She just had her baby."

"Goodness," Ali said. "Is everyone in this country pregnant or about to give birth?"

"You would know that better than me." One of Crystal's light brown eyebrows rose. "And don't try to sidetrack me. Why do you look like you're having the worst day of your life?"

Because every day since she'd realized Kamal didn't love her had been worse than the last. Eventually she would bottom out, emotionally speaking. When that happened, she would probably look as if she'd been run over by a herd of thirsty camels.

"Do I really look that bad?" she hedged.

"No," Crystal answered quickly.

Ali knew she was lying. She really thought she'd been successfully hiding her heartbreak. But maybe the strain of concealing her feelings had taken more of a toll than she'd realized.

"At breakfast this morning, Princess Farrah hinted that Kamal would be making an announcement soon about his intended bride."

"And this would pertain to me—how?"

The other woman lifted one shoulder. "I assumed you would want to know."

"I'll refrain from pointing out what happens when you *assume*. But why would you think I'd want to know he's engaged?"

"Oh, come on, Ali. Do you think no one can see the way you look at him?"

"What about the way he looks at me?" she countered.

"That, too. A blind fool could see he's in love with you."

"Then maybe it's just us twenty-twenty sighted re-alists who get that he won't let himself care."

The other woman snorted. "Let's go sit down," she suggested.

Ali nodded and they paid for their items, then selected a table that looked out on the memorial garden. Bad move, she thought. Scene of the crime. It was where Kamal had been her hero and she'd realized she was in love with him.

Ali settled herself with her back to the window. Across from her, Crystal sipped her herbal tea and looked beautiful. Was it just an old wives' tale that there was a glow about a pregnant woman? She figured she would never know. She wouldn't marry without love, which meant she wasn't likely to marry at all. Without marriage, she wouldn't have children. No one knew better than she did about the stigma and difficulties of being the child of a one-parent home. Or the one parent doing double duty. As badly as she wanted a baby, she wouldn't do that to her child.

"Now, then," Crystal said. "What's going on with you and Kamal?"

"Nothing. And I mean that literally."

"But I could have sworn romance was brewing."

"Did Princess Farrah say who his intended bride is?" Ali asked as nonchalantly as possible.

"No. And I assumed you would have something to say about it."

"There's that A-word again."

Crystal laughed. "Like I said, given our visual clues, it was logical. Come on. Fess up. You're sweet on him, aren't you?"

Ali sighed, then nodded miserably. "For all the good

it does me. He's a walking, talking cliché of the com-
mitment-phobic male.''

"I don't get it. I could have sworn he was falling
for you—as long as we're talking in clichés—like a
ton of bricks.''

"There's falling going on, but it's a one-sided brick
slide on me.''

Crystal shook her head. "Something's weird. When
the princess was doing all this hinting around, she was
grilling Penny and I about the courting practices of the
average male.''

Ali sat up straighter. "Why?''

"Because Penny and I are the peasants who married
into the royal family. I suppose we were her best research source and the only ones likely to know how a
regular guy would go about wooing.''

"No, I mean why did she want to know this information at all?''

Crystal shrugged. "I guess because Kamal is going
courting.''

Ali's chest felt as if a boulder was sitting on it, pressing against her heart. The smartest thing to do would
be to get on with her life and learn to live it without
him. Once he'd married, she hoped it would be an
achievable goal.

"Good for him,'' she said.

"I don't get it,'' Crystal said. "I thought you'd want
to fight for him.''

"Even if I did,'' Ali countered, "how could I? I've
got no weapons to fight with. I'm an average, ordinary
woman who has no business with anyone but an average, ordinary man.''

"Then we have to agree to disagree.'' Crystal toyed
with the handle of her teacup. "Because Penny and I

are pretty average, but we fell in love. Oddly enough, the men of our dreams loved us right back.''

Ali thought about her remark, that she and Penny were the peasants who married into the royal family. ''Just out of curiosity— What did you and Penny tell Princess Farrah about the courting rituals of the common male?''

A beautiful smile spread over the other woman's features. ''We told her in our experience dates to the bowling alley and the local pizza hangout were guaranteed to win a girl's heart.''

Ali stared at her, then started laughing. ''You guys are wicked.''

''Yeah.'' She chuckled. ''She took us seriously at first. Then we came clean and clued her in that we were teasing her.''

''So did you ever get serious?'' Ali asked.

Crystal nodded. ''We told her a man could never go wrong with flowers, candy and jewelry. The average guy falls back on those three things for the standard romantic gesture.''

''What did the princess say?''

''That she and the king had told Kamal exactly that.''

Ali sighed. ''Whatever technique he uses, I'm sure the woman he courts will dissolve in a puddle at his feet.''

''Probably. Besides not being average, that's another characteristic the Hassan men have in common. Goodness knows it happened to me.'' Crystal stood. ''And speaking of my husband, we have a romantic evening alone planned and I need to go. Take care, Ali.''

''You, too.''

"For what it's worth, I think you should fight for him. Go to Kamal and tell him how you feel."

Ali watched the other woman walk away. How she envied Crystal, a woman who had a man who adored her and a baby on the way. Ali's heart felt heavy as sadness settled over her. She liked and respected both Crystal and Penny. For a brief twelve-hour period, she'd enjoyed the idea of being their sister-in-law. But she couldn't take Crystal's advice. Kamal already knew how she felt and it changed nothing.

He couldn't love her.

Ali unlocked the door to her apartment, then closed it and put her salad in the fridge for later. She wasn't especially hungry, but then her appetite had taken the last two weeks off. Nothing about her life had been right since losing Kamal. And she wondered if anything about her would ever be right again.

There was always work and she loved it. But nursing wouldn't keep her bed warm at night.

Darn it. Talking to Crystal had really sent her into a downward spiral. But she had to snap out of it. She'd made the decision to stick it out here in El Zafir and that meant occasionally seeing members of the royal family. She couldn't lose it every time that happened.

Time to change out of work clothes and decide on something fun to do with her evening. Since her inclination was to put on pajamas and robe and curl into a fetal position, she donned jeans, a hunter-green sweater and fuzzy slippers. She had a bookcase full of romance novels she hadn't had time to read. If she couldn't have a hot-and-heavy love affair, by gosh she could read one. Or her video case held numerous romantic comedies. How pathetic was she?

There was a knock on her door, startling her. Kamal! She hated that his was the first name that popped into her mind. The cycle of hope, then disappointment followed by pain, could really do a number on a girl's forced cheerfulness.

She walked over to the door and stared wistfully up at the peephole for a moment. "Who is it?" she asked, and cursed the pesky part of her that yearned and hoped to hear Kamal's voice.

"I have a delivery." Definitely not Kamal.

Without removing the chain from its lock, she opened the door to look out. A man stood there with a flower arrangement. "There must be some mistake," she said.

"You are Miss Ali Matlock?"

"Yes, but—"

He glanced over his shoulder to someone behind him that she couldn't see. "Bring the rest."

She took the security chain off and opened the door. "The rest of what?"

The man walked past her and set the lovely arrangement of pink lilies, yellow mums, white carnations and baby's breath on her bar.

He looked at her. "There are more flowers."

"But who sent them?"

He motioned to three more men who carried in different colorful, fragrant and artfully arranged sprays.

"Is there a card?" she asked.

Instead of answering, he left with the others. Several moments later each came back with another arrangement. Finally, the man placed on her living-room coffee table what looked like two dozen of the most perfect red roses she'd ever seen.

"Here is the card," he said, handing her a small envelope with her name on it.

When they started to walk out, she said, "Wait. I need to give you something for your trouble."

He shook his head. "It's already been taken care of." Bowing slightly, he said, "Have a nice day."

Then they were gone and she was alone. But her apartment looked like a florist shop and smelled like a garden.

She slipped the small card from the envelope and read the words that were written in a familiar hand. "The beauty of these blossoms pales beside your loveliness. Kamal."

Ali's heart pounded against the wall of her chest. She was completely stunned. A trembling began and spread through her. Before she could sit down, there was another knock on the door.

"Kamal," she whispered.

She hurried to the entryway, but when she yanked open the door, a man she'd never seen stood there. "Miss Ali Matlock?"

"Y-yes," she said.

"I have a delivery for you." He handed her a gold-foil box with raised embossed lettering.

She looked down at the package in her hands. "What is it?"

He smiled. "It is a five-pound box of the finest Swiss chocolate. The crown prince had it flown in especially for you. It arrived a short while ago."

Golly. Flowers and now candy. What in the world was going on? The man started to turn away. "Wait. Let me get you something for your trouble—"

He held up a hand. "It's already been taken care of."

"Of course it has." She shook her head. "Thank you."

"You are most welcome. Have a nice day."

She closed the door and leaned against it. She was having a "day," but nice didn't seem adequate to describe it. Puzzling was more to the point. What was Kamal up to? She had no doubt that he had an agenda. Was he trying to buy her? For an affair? Or was he trying to bribe her into dropping her demand for love?

Another knock shocked her socks off and surprised a squeal out of her as she jumped away. She whirled and opened the door.

This time Kamal stood there with a box in his hands. It was leather and was the shape and size to hold silverware—a service for sixteen or more.

"Hello," he said.

"H-hi." She stared for several moments, just taking in the wonderful sight of him.

"Is there nothing else you have to say?"

She blinked as she looked up at him and shrugged. "I'm speechless."

"Such an occurrence should be declared a national holiday. I will see to it." One corner of his mouth curved upward.

"Very funny."

"May I come in?" he asked.

She glanced over her shoulder at the flowers everywhere. "I'm not sure there's room in here."

He brushed past her, looked around and nodded. "Excellent."

She shut the door and walked over to him. "Care for a piece of candy? It was just flown in from Switzerland."

"On my orders," he said, looking confused. "You are upset?"

"I don't know how I feel," she answered honestly. Nodding at the leather box in his hands, she said, "Don't tell me. You've got jewelry in there."

"Yes," he said proudly. "The royal jewels."

He looked around for a place to set down the box, but every available table held a flower arrangement. Finally he settled it on one of the bar stools. Lifting the wooden lid, he revealed a black-velvet-lined interior. On the soft material rested a diamond-encrusted tiara, a necklace made of sapphires and perfectly matched pearls, a diamond and emerald bracelet and ruby earrings.

"This is just a small part of the collection."

Ali's eyes grew wide. "I—I—"

"You are speechless again?" When she nodded, he asked, "How did you know this was jewelry?"

She swallowed hard. "Flowers, candy, jewelry—the cornerstone of the romantic gesture."

He nodded. "Just so."

She breathed deeply and the almost overpowering scent of flowers filled her head. She glared at him. "I don't get it."

He frowned. "The flowers do not please you?"

"Of course they please me. I love flowers."

"Then it is the candy. Tell me what is your favorite and I will have it brought—" He stopped and studied her. "You are still angry?"

She threw up her hands. "There's that have-you-stopped-beating-your-wife question again. If I say yes, I'm an ungrateful witch. If I say no, I'd be lying. I guess the best answer is I don't know how to feel. I don't know what to think. What do you want?"

"I wish for you to marry me." He nodded at the glittering, priceless jewels in the case. "These will belong to the woman who becomes my wife."

"Are you trying to buy me?"

He straightened, his back ramrod-stiff, and his gaze narrowed on her. "I do not understand how you could think such a thing."

She put the box of candy beside the roses on the living-room table. She needed distance from him. It would be too easy to grab the happiness he was dangling in front of her. Because, with every fiber of her being, she wanted to say yes. But she couldn't compromise her principles.

"What is all this about? What are you doing?" she asked.

"I am courting you. Is it not obvious?" He folded his arms over his chest and looked down. "I have been told that this is what the average man does when he is attempting to woo the woman of his choice."

"Who told you this?" It was a question to stall for time because she already knew the answer.

"My father and Aunt Farrah. And I did some research regarding this subject on the Internet," he said proudly.

He'd obviously gone to some trouble, in addition to picking up the phone and delegating. Which made her love him all the more. But it wasn't enough.

"How do you feel about me?" she asked.

His gaze darkened. "My study revealed that most women are satisfied with tangible tokens of affection. There is more credence in what a man does than in what he says."

"Show don't tell?"

"Exactly."

She took a deep breath. This was the point of no
return. If she couldn't make him understand, if she
turned him away, there wouldn't be a third time's the
charm. He was a proud man—a good man. But he
wouldn't ask her again. And she couldn't accept him
if he didn't love her. She prayed for the right words to
make him know that this was a deal breaker for her.

She worried her top lip between her teeth as she
twisted her fingers together. "Kamal, I want you to
know that I care for you very deeply." He started to
reach for her and she held up her hand and backed
away. "No. Let me finish. My father didn't love me.
He never told me and everything he did spoke loud
and clear that he was indifferent to me. He chose a
better wife and had a better family with her."

"He is an idiot."

She managed a small smile. "Then Turner did the
same thing. After we dated for several years, he picked
a better, more appropriate woman to be his wife. I love
you," she said. "But I can't marry you unless I'm
convinced that I'm your one and only. I need to hear
the words."

He let out a long breath and ran his fingers through
his hair. When he met her gaze his own smoldered with
emotion. "I am unaccustomed to such a thing."

"So I've discovered," she said.

"I have known many women," he said. "I do not
say this to hurt you, but it is a fact. Many have thrown
themselves at me for their own shallow, selfish pur-
poses. None of them was acceptable to me."

"I see," she said.

"There is more," he said. "As you know, it is my
wish to be a wise and strong ruler for my people. I
have discussed this problem with my father and he as-

sures me it is possible to guide my country and be with a woman. In fact, it is advisable to do so.''

She longed to kiss him at the same time she wanted to choke him. She wished he would either get on with it or put her out of her misery. "So you've decided that love isn't a weakness?" she prompted.

The corners of his mouth curved up slightly. "I could have had my pick among women."

"And your point would be?"

"You wish me to say that I love you, but I have little experience with this word." He moved to her and took her hands in his. When his gaze met hers, there was no humor there. He was completely serious and sincere. "But I can tell you this—you are unique among all the women I have known. You are special. You have touched a place inside me that no one else could reach. Without you there is no color in my world. When you turned away from me, you took the light and warmth with you. My world is empty without your joy and laughter, your wisdom and support. You have given me my soul and taken my heart. I beseech you not to take it without giving me yours in return. From my father I learned that to turn away from you would be a greater personal disaster than anything I can imagine.''

"Oh, Kamal—" He'd given her more than all the flowers, candy and jewels in the world could buy. She didn't need the L-word. His way had been far more eloquent, more heartfelt than she could ever have hoped.

Gently but firmly he squeezed her hands. "I cannot—I will not lose the love that you so freely give. I wish to give it in return. I love you, Ali. Be my wife.

Bear my children. Make me the happiest man in the world.''

She stared at him through a sudden veil of tears. "Yes," she whispered.

He closed his eyes for a moment as he let out a long breath. "This was what you wished to hear?"

"Oh, yes," she said. "You don't do anything half-way, do you?" She looked around at the flowers filling her apartment and laughed.

"You can settle for a man who is not a regular, average, ordinary man?"

She nodded, dislodging the tears gathered in her eyes. "It's not settling if he's you."

"I will make you happy." He cupped her face in his hands, brushing the moisture from her cheeks with his thumbs. "Do not cry, my love."

He touched his lips to hers in a too-brief, achingly tender kiss.

When he lifted his head, she smiled up at him. "I'm not crying. Not exactly. It's just happiness spilling over."

"I hope you do not intend to spend the rest of our lives crying. You must accustom yourself to this feeling, because I will make it so every day."

"And I will do the same for you."

Ali wondered if this was what it felt like to win the lottery. If so, it was the lottery of love. Her numbers had come up; her dreams had come true. She couldn't think of anything that would make her happier than being loved by this extraordinary man.

Epilogue

Kamal watched his three-day-old son suckle at Ali's breast. The sight aroused in him so many emotions— gratitude, contentment, exhilaration, pride, but most of all love. Ali was his wife, friend, lover, and now the mother of his child. Khadeem. Even as she dozed in the act of feeding the infant from her body, she held the baby with an instinctive nurturing strength that never failed to awe and inspire him.

Her eyes fluttered open and when she saw him, a lovely smile curved the corners of her mouth. "Hi."

"Hello." He sat on the side of their bed, his thigh brushing hers. "I did not mean to disturb you."

Taking her free hand, he placed a kiss on her knuckles, then rubbed his thumb over the large emerald ring nestled against the plain gold band proclaiming for all the world to see that she was his—only his. The thought never failed to please him.

"You didn't disturb me." She squeezed his fingers

and blessed him with a love-filled look. "I miss you when you're not here."

"And I you. He is a good eater, our son," he said, nodding at the dark-haired baby who was sleeping peacefully.

"Yes," she agreed. "He eats well—and often."

He frowned as he studied the dark circles beneath her eyes. In spite of reassurances that the best medical care was available in the hospital he'd built, he'd worried during her pregnancy. Ali had known he would and had done her best to calm his fears. The birth had been without complication, for which he was grateful.

He trailed a finger over her cheek. "I know you prefer to tend him yourself, but—"

"You're sweet to worry about me, but please don't. If I need help, I'll ask," she assured him.

"I love you," he said.

She smiled. "I never get tired of hearing you say so."

"That is good, because I plan to say it often."

The lesson had been long and difficult for him, but he'd finally learned it. His father's weakness wasn't in loving well. If he'd been guilty of any fault, it was a lapse in judgment. Kamal was easing into his father's duties, but he would do his best not to make the same mistakes. When the king retired in a few months, he would take over leadership of his people. Life did not come with a guarantee and he planned to live each day to the fullest with his wife and son. If they were blessed with more children, there would be plenty of love to go around.

"Would you like to hold him?" she asked.

"Yes."

Ali shifted the infant into her husband's strong arms.

She knew he'd grown accustomed to the feel of babies after the births of his brothers' children. The healthy baby girls had been born a month apart.

Kamal met her gaze, then stared at his son with an awed expression. "The rest of his family is here to see him."

"And what am I? Chopped liver?"

"Never," he said, amusement in his gaze when he met her. "But I will tell them you are too tired for visitors just yet."

"But I'm not," she protested. "I want to see everyone. They're my family, too."

And she would never take them for granted. For too long she'd felt alone in the world. But not anymore. The royal family had not only orchestrated her romance with the sheik of her dreams, they'd welcomed her with open arms. She would never let them down.

"All right." He stood with the baby in his arms. "They are all waiting in the living room. I love you," he said again before leaving her.

Ali slipped out of bed to put on her robe. Third day postpartum she was feeling much better, although her body was still a bit sore. But happiness canceled out pain. Her heart swelled with love for her husband and child. Kamal had been a pillar of strength through her pregnancy.

She'd worried that the sight of her body growing large would bother him. As always, he'd shown her in word and deed that she was more beautiful to him. Thanks to him, she would never again doubt her value. She looked back on the time before their marriage and gave thanks for the bad experiences. Knowing a few wrong men had prepared her to be grateful when she'd met the right one.

She walked out into the living room. Princess Farrah was sitting on the couch holding the baby. Rafiq and Penny sat on one side of her with their baby girl, Fareeza. On the other side were Crystal and Fariq with their baby, Janeen, and their six-year-old twins. Hana and Nuri were delighted with all their new cousins. The king stood nearby, beaming at everyone. He had reconciled with Johara and when he retired, planned a trip to Texas to see her and his grandson.

Ali had gained a husband and son. She had brothers and sisters and nieces and a nephew.

Kamal moved beside her and slipped his arm around her waist. She leaned into his warmth and strength.

"Do you ever regret what you've gotten yourself into?" he whispered in her ear.

She shook her head and smiled up at him. "Never."

"Have I thanked you for my son?"

She thought of the necklace he'd given her with a single flawless diamond and a promise for another with the next child. "Yes, you did."

He nodded at his child in the arms of his great-aunt. "You and I will guide the country through the infancy of the new millennium. Are you ready?"

"Yes. Together we can do anything," she said. "Maybe even convince you to admit you're sometimes wrong."

"Never." He grinned. "Especially about the fact that you would make an exemplary wife, mother and queen. So you are not sorry you said yes?"

"Never. The thought of living without you was too awful to contemplate. I will never regret my decision to wed a sheik."

*   *   *   *   *

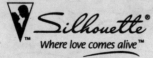

If you enjoyed what you just read,
then we've got an offer you can't resist!

Take 2 bestselling
love stories FREE!

Plus get a FREE surprise gift!

Clip this page and mail it to Silhouette Reader Service

IN U.S.A.	IN CANADA
3010 Walden Ave.	P.O. Box 609
P.O. Box 1867	Fort Erie, Ontario
Buffalo, N.Y. 14240-1867	L2A 5X3

YES! Please send me 2 free Silhouette Romance® novels and my free surprise gift. After receiving them, if I don't wish to receive anymore, I can return the shipping statement marked cancel. If I don't cancel, I will receive 6 brand-new novels every month, before they're available in stores! In the U.S.A., bill me at the bargain price of $21.34 per shipment plus 25¢ shipping and handling per book and applicable sales tax, if any*. In Canada, bill me at the bargain price of $24.68 plus 25¢ shipping and handling per book and applicable taxes**. That's the complete price and a savings of at least 10% off the cover prices—what a great deal! I understand that accepting the 2 free books and gift places me under no obligation ever to buy any books. I can always return a shipment and cancel at any time. Even if I never buy another book from Silhouette, the 2 free books and gift are mine to keep forever.

209 SDN DU9H
309 SDN DU9J

Name	(PLEASE PRINT)
Address	Apt.#
City	State/Prov. Zip/Postal Code

* Terms and prices subject to change without notice. Sales tax applicable in N.Y.
** Canadian residents will be charged applicable provincial taxes and GST.
 All orders subject to approval. Offer limited to one per household and not valid to current Silhouette Romance® subscribers.
® are registered trademarks of Harlequin Books S.A., used under license.

SROM03   ©1998 Harlequin Enterprises Limited

Your opinion is important to us! Please take a few moments to share your thoughts with us about your experiences with Harlequin and Silhouette books. Your comments will be very useful in ensuring that we deliver books you love to read. *Please take a few minutes to complete the questionnaire, then send it to us at the address below.*

Send your completed questionnaires to:
Harlequin/Silhouette Reader Survey, P.O. Box 9046, Buffalo, NY 14269-9046

1. As you may know, there are many different lines under the Harlequin and Silhouette brands. Each of the lines is listed below. Please check the box that most represents your reading habit for each line.

Line	Currently read this line	Do not read this line	Not sure if I read this line
Harlequin American Romance	❏	❏	❏
Harlequin Duets	❏	❏	❏
Harlequin Romance	❏	❏	❏
Harlequin Historicals	❏	❏	❏
Harlequin Superromance	❏	❏	❏
Harlequin Intrigue	❏	❏	❏
Harlequin Presents	❏	❏	❏
Harlequin Temptation	❏	❏	❏
Harlequin Blaze	❏	❏	❏
Silhouette Special Edition	❏	❏	❏
Silhouette Romance	❏	❏	❏
Silhouette Intimate Moments	❏	❏	❏
Silhouette Desire	❏	❏	❏

2. Which of the following best describes why you bought *this book?* One answer only, please.

the picture on the cover ❏   the title ❏
the author ❏   the line is one I read often ❏
part of a miniseries ❏   saw an ad in another book ❏
saw an ad in a magazine/newsletter ❏   a friend told me about it ❏
I borrowed/was given this book ❏   other: _____ ❏

3. Where did you buy *this book?* One answer only, please.

at Barnes & Noble ❏   at a grocery store ❏
at Waldenbooks ❏   at a drugstore ❏
at Borders ❏   on eHarlequin.com Web site ❏
at another bookstore ❏   from another Web site ❏
at Wal-Mart ❏   Harlequin/Silhouette Reader ❏
at Target ❏   Service/through the mail
at Kmart ❏   used books from anywhere ❏
at another department store ❏   I borrowed/was given this ❏
or mass merchandiser   book

4. On average, how many Harlequin and Silhouette books do you buy at one time?

I buy _____ books at one time ❏
I rarely buy a book ❏

MRQ403SR-1A

5. How many times per month do you shop for any *Harlequin and/or Silhouette* books?
   One answer only, please.

1 or more times a week	❏	a few times per year	❏
1 to 3 times per month	❏	less often than once a year	❏
1 to 2 times every 3 months	❏	never	❏

6. When you think of your ideal heroine, which *one* statement describes her the best?
   One answer only, please.

She's a woman who is strong-willed	❏	She's a desirable woman	❏
She's a woman who is needed by others	❏	She's a powerful woman	❏
She's a woman who is taken care of	❏	She's a passionate woman	❏
She's an adventurous woman	❏	She's a sensitive woman	❏

7. The following statements describe types or genres of books that you may be
   interested in reading. Pick *up to 2 types* of books that you are most interested in.

I like to read about truly romantic relationships	❏
I like to read stories that are sexy romances	❏
I like to read romantic comedies	❏
I like to read a romantic mystery/suspense	❏
I like to read about romantic adventures	❏
I like to read romance stories that involve family	❏
I like to read about a romance in times or places that I have never seen	❏
Other: _____	❏

*The following questions help us to group your answers with those readers who are
similar to you. Your answers will remain confidential.*

8. Please record your year of birth below.

   19 ____

9. What is your marital status?

   single ❏   married ❏   common-law ❏   widowed ❏
   divorced/separated ❏

10. Do you have children 18 years of age or younger currently living at home?

    yes ❏   no ❏

11. Which of the following best describes your employment status?

    employed full-time or part-time ❏   homemaker ❏   student ❏
    retired ❏   unemployed ❏

12. Do you have access to the Internet from either home or work?

    yes ❏   no ❏

13. Have you ever visited eHarlequin.com?

    yes ❏   no ❏

14. What state do you live in?

    _____

15. Are you a member of Harlequin/Silhouette Reader Service?

    yes ❏   Account # _____   no ❏   MRQ403SR-1B

SILHOUETTE *Romance*

COMING NEXT MONTH

#1698 SANTA BROUGHT A SON—Melissa McClone
Marrying the Boss's Daughter

An old friend's wedding had brought Reed Connors back
home—and face-to-face with Samantha Wilson. Determined
not to let the one-who-got-away get away a second time, he
vowed to win her heart. But then he met Samantha's young son
whose striking resemblance to Reed was undeniable. Had Santa
brought the lonely VP the most precious gift of all: a family?

#1699 THE PRINCE & THE MARRIAGE PACT—
Valerie Parv
The Carramer Trust

Annegret West was unimpressed with titled men and
majestic trappings, but somehow His Royal Heartthrob
Prince Maxim de Marigny made her jaded heart flutter! Yet
despite her growing emotional attachment, she knew Maxim
must marry a princess or forfeit his throne. If only she had
been born royal....

#1700 THE BACHELOR'S DARE—Shirley Jump

Ladies' man Mark Dole and down-on-her-luck Claire Richards
both had the same goal: win the "Survive and Drive" contest's
grand prize, an RV, to fund their future dreams. But could these
childhood enemies put aside their competitive natures and
work together to win? And would a crazy contest end with
good old-fashioned romance in an RV for the playboy and the
hairdresser?

#1701 THE NANNY'S PLAN—Donna Clayton

Workaholic professor Pierce Kincaid may have agreed to
baby-sit his six-year-old nephews for the summer, but he certainly wasn't going to do it alone! Enter Amy Edwards,
the temporary take-charge nanny he hired to tame the rambunc-
tious twins. It looked like Pierce's not-so-quiet summer was
going to be an adventure in life—and love!

SRCNM1103